A Festive Feud

MAREN MOORE

Cover Design: Maren Moore
Artist: Chelsea Kemp
Editing: One Love Editing
Proofread: Sarah P.

A Strawberry Hollow Novella

A Note from Maren

A FESTIVE FEUD IS A 49,000 WORD NOVELLA PACKED FULL OF SPICE AND ALL THE CHRISTMAS FEELINGS TO PUT YOU IN THE SPIRIT THIS YEAR!

THIS BOOK IS MEANT TO MAKE YOU FEEL LIKE YOU'RE WATCHING A BELOVED HALLMARK MOVIE, BUT ADD IN ALL THE THINGS WE NEVER GOT! :)

MERRY CHRISTMAS!

XO MAREN

THIS IS FOR ALL THE GIRLS ON SANTA'S NAUGHTY LIST WHO WISHED THEIR HALLMARK MOVIES HAD A DASH OF SPICE, AND A PINCH OF TENSION.

Welcome to Hallmark after dark.

1 /

emma

Santa, I'm in love with a criminal

I love Christmas *almost* as much as I loathe Jackson Pearce. That's saying a lot since Christmas is *magical*.

There's just something… whimsical about the snow falling, lights twinkling along the Christmas tree, the smell of pine and fir fresh in the air. Traditions and family. The excitement you feel when you wake up on Christmas morning and rush to the tree. The sense of innocence and wonder that you hold on to well past your childhood years.

Yet somehow, Jackson Pearce *still* manages to ruin all of that.

"Emmie," he says, an arrogant smirk tugging at the corner of his full lips. One that I immediately want to wipe right off his stupidly handsome face.

Even *I* can't deny that the man is unfairly attractive. Even if I want to hit him with my car.

He's tall, at least over six foot three if I had to guess, with deep chestnut-colored hair and stubble to match. High cheekbones, warm whiskey eyes, a strong, sharp jaw. He's always been handsome, and truthfully, it only makes me detest him more.

How dare he be so attractive and yet the most annoying man to ever walk the planet.

And how absolutely rude of fate and the universe to put us together in Strawberry Hollow, which at times feels like the tiniest small town in America.

"It's *Emma*," I respond through clenched teeth. "I *hate* that you call me that."

"I know." He chuckles, plucking a stuffed Santa off the shelf and twirling it in his hand. I try not to watch the thick muscles of his forearms ripple as he does. He's got the whole "roll up the sleeves of my flannel to show off my hot, veiny forearms" thing down to a science. "Why do you think I do it?"

Rolling my eyes, I step away, ready to rid myself of this conversation and *him* as soon as possible.

All I wanted was to come to the general store today to pick up the limited edition nutcracker that I have been so patiently—okay, fine, *not* so patiently—waiting to arrive, and because apparently I've been on the naughty list, I've run into Jackson in the process.

It's not just that he does whatever he possibly can to push my buttons, or the fact that his ego is the size of Town Square, or even that he calls me Emmie just to make my blood boil that makes me absolutely loathe him.

Sure, all of those things add to the already burning fire.

But the real reason that Jackson Pearce and I hate each other has everything to do with the fact that our families have been enemies for decades.

The Pearces vs the Worthingtons.

Our long-standing feud has gone back for over thirty years, starting when our parents first met.

The small-town version of the Capulets and the Montagues.

The Hatfields and the McCoys.

Jack Frost and Santa Claus.

The Grinch and the Who.

A rivalry that has withstood time and, at some points, rational thinking.

So even if he wasn't enemy number one for all of those reasons I listed, we were born to hate each other.

He just simply makes it easier to do so.

"What brings you out of the mansion, Emmie?" He invades my space once more, and I get a whiff of whatever cologne he's wearing. Bergamot and warm amber. Spice.

He smells delicious.

Add that to the list of things I hate about him.

"It's none of your bus—"

"Oh, she's here about the new nutcracker! Goodness, you know, I can't keep those things in stock. It's a shame—the manufacturer says it's the last restock of the season." Sweet, dear old Clara gestures to the lone nutcracker on the shelf, and my eyes widen.

No. No. No. *No*. Please, no.

This cannot be happening.

My eyes flit back to Jackson, whose brow is raised in question. For a moment, neither of us moves.

We engage in a silent stare-off.

His eyes dart from mine to the decoration and back, and it's as if I can read his thoughts.

I know exactly where this is going, which is why I'm the

first to move, launching myself at the shelf so I can grab it first.

Except, of course, it doesn't work that way. Why would *anything* be easy when he's involved?

Both of us grab on to the nutcracker at the same time, our gazes locked on each other as we each hold on with no plans to let go.

"Put it down, *Pearce*," I whisper-yell as I yank it toward me.

He tugs it back toward him, pulling me along with it. "In your dreams, *Emmie*."

Yank. "God, you are the most annoying man I've ever met. Like you actually care about this damn nutcracker. You clearly only want it because *I* want it."

"No, I want it because it would be perfect for our Christmas party. You know not everything is about *you*, right?"

Tug.

Scoffing, I pull harder, yanking it back toward me in this ridiculous game of tug-of-war that we're engaging in. "Oh, that's fresh, coming from *you*. I'm surprised that your ego can even fit inside this building."

"Funny, because your 'too good for everyone' attitude makes it feel a *bit* stuffy in here," he retorts.

Tug.

Pull.

Yank.

"This is childish. Let go, Emmie. Be the bigger person."

"Never, Pearce."

This time, I yank harder than I have yet and lose my

footing as I bump into the display behind me. I can feel the air in the room shift before it even happens.

The entire store has gone deathly quiet, and seconds later, there's the telltale clink of glass as the entire display behind me falls backward and plummets to the floor in a deafening shatter.

Oh. My. God.

A few seconds pass where I'm too afraid to move, like if I do, then I might further the already catastrophic damage that has ensued. Exhaling, I drop the nutcracker as if it's on fire, my eyes widened in shock as I slowly turn toward the ruins.

Glass ornaments are scattered along the floor in a heap of broken shards.

There are so many of them you can hardly see the floor beneath it.

My eyes dart to Clara's, her jaw agape in shock and a worrisome dip between her brows, her hand clutched to her chest like she needs to hold on to her heart. Slowly, her hand moves toward the ancient turn-dial phone next to her, and she lifts the receiver, dialing three numbers.

That's when I realize just how screwed we are, and it's *all* because of Jackson Pearce.

"WAYNE, come on. You've known me since I was in *diapers*. This feels a little extreme for just a minor… little disagreement," I mutter.

Wayne scoffs, shaking his head as he adjusts his hat lower, his shiny sheriff's badge glinting beneath the light of the general store. "Minor, Emma? You two"—he points between Jackson and me—"destroyed over ten thousand dollars' worth of merchandise! Let's not even get into the mess that poor Clara is going to have to deal with since the two of you are spending the night in lockup. You almost gave that sweet old lady a heart attack."

My jaw drops.

Lockup? As in… *jail*?

Not that Strawberry Hollow has an actual jail. It's more of just a small four-by-four cell with an old rusty door.

But still…

Surely he's not actually going to put me in a cell like some kind of… *criminal*. Wait until my parents hear about this. They might literally kill me.

"You're throwing us in the drunk tank? We're not even drunk, Wayne!" Jackson groans. "Come on, man. For once in my life, I have to agree with Emmie. We got into a small disagreement, and accidents happen. You know that. We'll pay for the damages and get everything cleaned up."

"Sure, I do." Wayne nods, crossing his arms over his chest. "But this was no dang accident, Jackson. Look, we've all had enough."

He pinches the bridge of his nose, exhaling as his eyes fall shut. When he opens them, they're filled to the brim with frustration. "Both of your families have been at this for years, and everyone in the town has had about enough of it. I mean it. You've given me no other choice."

I can see Jackson shake his head beside me before he retorts, "Yeah? This is going to make for a great conversation at the next poker night. Share a beer and tell all the guys about how you threw me in jail for fighting with Emmie Worthington."

I snort.

Of course, Jackson Pearce would play poker with the sheriff. Too bad that little detail isn't helping in this situation since we're about to spend the night in jail all because he's got the maturity level of a teenage boy.

Some of us have grown up, but he's obviously still the same immature boy from when we were in school.

Clearly, this is all of his fault.

If he would've just let go of the stupid nutcracker and left me the hell alone, then none of this would have happened in the first place.

But no, he had to go and try and one-up me, as he and his family *always* have done.

"Yeah, well, maybe both of you shouldn't have gotten into a fight in the middle of the general store and broken a whole bunch of shit, then, huh? Now, let's go. Don't make me handcuff you."

My eyes widen as panic rises in my throat. "You... wouldn't."

His brows rise. "Try me."

Great.

Add felon to the list of my most attractive qualities.

2 /
jackson

You're a mean one, Jackson Pearce

T he sound of the metal door slamming shut echoes throughout the concrete walls, a deafening sound that has an air of finality to it. My gaze meets Wayne's, and I just shake my head, pushing off the bars in annoyance.

That fucking asshole *actually* put me in jail.

I didn't think he actually had the balls to do it, and he sure as hell proved me wrong.

Emma sighs behind me, and when I turn to face her, she's got her arms crossed over her chest, the tight fabric of her emerald-green sweater clinging to her in a way that I shouldn't notice. But then again, when have I ever *not* noticed Emma Worthington?

She's impossible not to notice. Even if she's my enemy by birthright.

Her long, honey-blonde hair falls in silky curls down to her waist. The red on her lips has faded slightly but makes her pouty lips no less kissable. Her bright blue eyes are framed by long, thick, dark lashes that kiss her eyelids.

She's more than beautiful. She's the kind of beautiful that sucks out all the air in a room the moment she enters.

Fuck, I hate that I'm attracted to her. She's the last person I should ever want, yet... I can't help that I do. Not that I'd ever be admitting that out loud to anyone. Nah, that shit is staying locked away in my brain safely where the *ice princess* can't wield my weakness as a weapon against me.

That is absolutely something she would do.

"You know this is all *your* fault, right?" She huffs, leaning against the back of the concrete cell. It's bad enough that the cell itself is the size of a small closet, but there's only a single bench that sits to the side, roughly a few feet long.

Clearly, this place wasn't built for comfort. But I guess a jail cell isn't supposed to be comfortable.

"My fault?" I scoff. "Sorry, Ice Princess, but had you not tried to fight me over a damn Christmas decoration, then we wouldn't be here right now. You could be in your mansion, sipping your expensive wine, clutching your pearls, and pretending that the world is perfect."

She laughs, the sound forced and lacking any real amusement. "I know you, Jackson Pearce. I'm not surprised at all that you'd stoop so low. Let me guess, this is some elaborate plan to ruin our party? Buying decor you don't even like so we can't have it. That seems very on brand for you. What a very *Pearce* thing to do. You heard that my parents have now passed the party down to me, and you're out to sabotage me. Fuck me, right?"

Christ. Here we fucking go.

It all goes back to the godforsaken *parties*. Every damn time.

The Worthingtons and Pearces have been at odds for years

over our competing town Christmas parties, so our mutual aversion for one another is always amplified during the holiday season.

But what started it all?

The fact that *our* family never got invited to their generations-old annual Christmas party when everyone else in the town was included. My parents had just moved to Strawberry Hollow. New to town and not invited to the town Christmas party. Clearly, the Worthingtons didn't want newcomers at their party. It was a very cold *welcome* to their new town, and so, the next year, my parents, who wanted to have their *own* Christmas celebration, threw their *own* party on the very same day and didn't invite the Worthingtons. Which is something *the Worthingtons* have never gotten over, especially since now half the town attends our parties instead. It's been like that every day since—tit for tat.

And thus, this not-so-friendly feud was born.

Immature and excessive? Definitely.

Trivial?

Probably so, but things are different when you live in a small town.

Truthfully, I have no idea why they never invited my parents, but they've snubbed my family at every turn. Ever since that first year, our families have made it their mission to "one-up" the other with our holiday parties, both families taking great effort to make their party the better one—better food, better fun, better traditions.

The tension has only gotten thicker between our families over the years, and somewhere along the way, a bit of sabotage got added to the one-upping. My siblings and I have partaken in... some *pranks* on the Worthingtons and their party preparations, a youthful tradition that we still enjoy as adults. One year, my brother Jameson filled their mailbox with coal, and there was that year in high school that we stuck forks in their yard the day of their party. We've stolen Christmas decorations, which we of course returned later, and we may have even built some naughty snowmen in their yard as teens. The Worthingtons have always retaliated, in their own way. They've tried to have our party permits revoked several times, sent the town police on a noise complaint, and Mr. Worthington has even gone so far as to use his connections at the electric company to cut our power one year.

At this point, most of the town has taken sides, and it makes the holidays stressful as fuck.

It's ridiculous when you *actually* say it out loud. Two families throwing parties just to outshine the other. Like copying each other's theme to see who can do it better. Or who can get more of the town to come by offering better food and an open bar. Nothing is off-limits when it comes to this party, and that's exactly the problem.

It just so happens that this year, the torch was passed down to us from our parents. So of course, the first year we're responsible for throwing the damn party, we end up in jail over a fucking *nutcracker.*

But honestly, me?

I don't give a shit about the stupid feud with the Worthingtons. Not *really*. The only thing that matters to me is Ma, and unfortunately, she *does* care about the stupid feud and our epic parties, which in turn makes me have to pretend that I'm so bothered that we're not included in their uptight, lavish cocktail party where the champagne alone costs more than what my company makes in a month.

If my family wasn't so invested, I wouldn't give a shit about any of it. But I have to admit, I love messing with Emma Worthington, to drive her as crazy as she does me. I want to push every button she has just to get a rise out of her.

I've always liked this… *game* between the two of us. This delicious tension that makes my dick hard.

She just thinks it has to do with our families hating each other. But the truth is, I don't actually hate Emma Worthington. I just want to shove my cock between her lips to shut her up.

"Don't flatter yourself into thinking I care that much. Not everything is about you. I know it's hard to think of the world not revolving around you, but it doesn't," I tell her, ignoring the sneer she throws my way as I walk past her to the concrete bench and take a seat. I cross my arms over my chest, lean back against the bars, and shut my eyes.

As much as I like fucking with her, I don't particularly like being stuck in a jail cell that smells like mildew and faintly of piss.

"This is going to be the longest night of my life," she mutters, more to herself than to me, I think.

I hum in response but keep my eyes shut. "I'm stuck in here with you too, Emmie."

"*Emma.*" I can hear the annoyance in her tone, and it makes my lips tug up into a smirk. "God, you're a pain in the ass."

Cracking one eye open, I see her shuffling from one foot to the other, and my gaze flicks down to her feet. She's wearing ridiculous black heels that make absolutely no sense with the amount of snow that's currently on the ground outside.

"You know there's another side of this bench for you to sit on, right?" I say, gesturing to the spot next to me. "I don't bite. Well... depends on who you ask."

"You're disgusting, and this entire place smells like pee. I'm not sitting on any surface in this place."

I shrug, dropping my head back. "Suit yourself."

Silence hangs in the air between us for a few minutes, even though I expected her to have a smart-ass reply to what I said.

"Are you really going to sit there... and not offer your shirt or something for me to at least sit on? That's what a *gentleman* would do, Pearce."

Sighing heavily, I sit up as I drag my hand through my hair, then stand from the bench. In two short strides, I close the distance between us, my hand finding a spot on the cell wall next to her head as I peer down at her. "And whatever gave you the impression that *I'm* a gentleman?"

The wide, shocked look in her eyes makes me deliriously fucking happy, and her plump lips open, then close. As if she might say something, but she's trying to find the right insult to throw my way.

For the first time, maybe ever, I've shut Emma Worthington up.

Unfortunately for me, it's not with my cock, but a win is a win.

"You're an *asshole*, you know that?"

"And you're a pretentious ice princess, but I think it's a waste of time to talk about the shit we already know, isn't it?"

Her lips flatten and then twist into a scowl as she looks

up at me through her thick lashes. She's short, but thanks to her ridiculous heels, there's only a few inches between us. My head dips lower to respond to whatever insult she'll spew, and she rises ever so slightly on her toes to reach my height.

Call it what you want, but I think she just might want me to kiss her as badly as I want to kiss her right now.

Thick tension fills the air. A beat passes with neither of us speaking. Moving. Breathing.

Then, I lean in a little further, but right before I meet her lips, I turn toward her ear to murmur, "I am an asshole, and I'm sure as fuck *not* a gentleman, so let's not pretend that I am."

With that, I push off the wall and walk back over to the bench. Before I sit down, I unbutton the flannel I'm wearing and shrug it off, leaving me in my white T-shirt decorated with holes. I spent the majority of the day on a jobsite, so it's the best I have.

Looking directly at Emma, I smirk as I spread it out on her side of the bench. "I'm only doing this so I don't have to spend the next eight hours listening to you complain about how bad your feet hurt in those things."

My gaze drops to her feet, and she huffs, "These are *Valentino*."

"And this is Ariat. Now, sit the fuck down before you get blisters. Some of us want some peace and quiet around here."

The daggers her eyes are shooting my way tell me just how much she wants to hit me, and I'm honestly a little surprised. It takes a lot to push her buttons this far, so she must have really wanted that damn nutcracker for her to be *this* angry.

She chews her lip for a moment, shifting from one foot to the other, wincing as she does.

"God, I hate you so much," she mutters, stomping over to the bench and sitting down gracefully next to me on top of my shirt. It's comical how *prissy* she is.

Her spine is rigid straight, and her hands are resting in her lap as she scoots to the very edge of the bench, as far as she possibly can away from me. Like being in such close proximity to me is going to cause her to catch whatever asshole funk I have.

We sit in a stiff silence for a while until she speaks. "Thank you. You're still a dick, but... thank you."

"Don't mention it."

"I won't, ever again. But I figured what happens in jail stays in jail, so maybe we can call somewhat of a... ceasefire? At least until we get out of here, and then I can go back to hating you with everything I have, and you can go back to annoying me to the ends of the earth."

Opening my eyes, I look over at her, her posture much more relaxed than when she first sat down, whether it be because she's exhausted or because she's tired of acting so damn uptight.

"Fine with me."

"Good." Her blonde curls bounce as she gives me a stiff nod.

I sit back again, crossing my arms over my chest, the cold metal of the bars biting through the thin T-shirt.

Fuck, it's cold and drafty in here.

My gaze travels to the clock, and I see that it's almost 10:30 p.m., which means we've been here for almost four hours after booking, with at least another eight hours to go if we're lucky.

That means another eight hours of pretending that I didn't *almost* kiss Emma Worthington and another eight hours of pretending that I still don't want to.

3 /

emma

Santa tell me... that this is a joke.

J ackson Pearce is haunting me, even in my dreams. Go figure, I can't escape him in the one tiny sliver of time that's solely mine and mine alone. He invades my thoughts and makes them his own.

I can practically smell his fresh, earthy scent that comes from long hours working in the sun with his bare hands. Practically feel the warmth of his skin on mine, how unwaveringly strong his muscles are beneath my touch.

Wait.

Wait.

Wait.

This feels entirely too *real* to be a dream.

I wake with a start, a gasp tumbling from my lips as my eyes crack open groggily. For a second, I forget that I'm sitting on this impossibly hard concrete bench inside a jail cell because I'm draped across a chest, and it's much softer than the bench yet still hard from the planes of muscles.

Oh *God*.

I'm lying across Jackson like he's a thousand-count

Egyptian cotton. Maybe if I don't move, he won't realize that I've woken up, and we can avoid this embarrassing situation entirely. It's not like I *meant* to fall asleep on top of him. Clearly, it happened in an act of subconsciousness.

"Don't worry, Emmie. Most women can't help but want to wake up on top of me."

His chest rumbles beneath me as he chuckles, and I sit up abruptly, almost falling off the side of this stupid, tiny bench.

"Clearly, I was asleep and had no idea what I was doing, or I would've chosen the floor over you," I scoff, brushing my fingers through my messy hair. My curls are limp and tangled from sleeping, and I can't imagine what my makeup must look like after hours in this concrete hell.

I can't wait to get out of here. To my own bed, in my own space, and to never have to think of this night or him ever again.

"I'm pretty sure you moaned my name in your sleep." He smirks. "Wouldn't be the first time though."

"I loathe you."

He shrugs. "Feeling is mutual, Emmie."

Standing from the bench, I cross to the other side of the cell and lean against the cold metal, my gaze narrowed on him.

I don't know how much longer I can take being stuck in this room with him before one of us kills the other.

So much for a ceasefire. Not that I expected it to *actually* happen. Wishful thinking.

When I woke up this morning, the very last thing I expected to happen was to end the night in a four-by-four jail cell with the most annoying man on the planet, yet I've learned in this short time that it is actually possible to hate someone more than you ever imagined.

And truly, there's not enough room between these concrete walls for both us and his ridiculously large ego.

It takes up most of the room, leaving no space for anything else.

We stay that way, both of us silently glaring at the other from across this small cell until I hear the sound of keys jangling, and my gaze flits to the door. Seconds later, Wayne appears, a wide smile on his face.

"Well, good morning to Strawberry Hollow's newest criminals. Sleep well? I hope our amenities were well suited for the two of you." He smiles smugly.

Jackson rises, stretching his arms above his head, a deep groan rumbling in his chest. I refuse to let my gaze drop to the sliver of skin that peeks out from the hem of his white tee and the waistband of his worn Wranglers.

"I've slept in worse places. Princess here, well, you know, she barely survived and probably wouldn't have if not for my gentlemanly ways. And they say chivalry is dead." Tossing me a shit-eating smirk, he swipes his flannel off the bench and shrugs it on, leaving it open, only rolling up the sleeves.

So rough and casual, nothing fancy or grandiose about him, but I can't pull my eyes away, as much as it irks me. I shouldn't be eyeing the man I hate, but here I am, ogling him like he's Sunday dinner.

"Get me out of here, Wayne. Please. Valentino is *not* meant for a jail cell," I mutter as I come to my senses, brushing past Jackson with a scowl.

My feet are hurting so badly I could actually cry, but I refuse to let my bare skin touch anything in this place for fear of getting hepatitis or something worse, and I'm not going to give Jackson the satisfaction of being right.

"Woah, woah, woah, Emma. Now, hold on a second. Mayor Davis is here in the lobby to see both of you." Wayne's expression sobers, and the smile he wore only a minute ago is nowhere to be seen. "I'm supposed to escort you out to sign your discharge paperwork and to meet with him. Come with me, please."

Jackson sighs but says nothing and gestures for me to go after Wayne. We walk down the dark, musty hallway of the tiny police station to the front waiting room that's not much bigger than the cell we just left.

"Ah, Jackson Pearce, Emma Worthington." Mayor Davis greets us both from the other side of the front desk. He's a short, balding, pudgy man with a kind smile and a combover. I've known him since I was a child.

Smiling, I offer him a tired wave. "Good morning, Mr. Davis."

"Jed." Jackson nods.

"Must say, I was not all that shocked to receive the phone call I did yesterday evening from Wayne, and I'm so disappointed in both of you. Quite frankly, myself, along with the rest of our town, is over your... *antics*. This has gone too far. Your families have been at each other's throats over this silly feud for too long."

"Mr. Davis, I—"

He holds his hand up, silencing me, and I can tell by the stern expression on his face that he is not interested in anything I have to say. And judging by the way Jackson's running his fingers through his already disheveled hair, he's as tense as I am.

"Yesterday was simply the gust that blew the house over. I'm done, Sheriff Williams is done. And this?" He gestures his pudgy finger between the both of us. "Is done. So here is what's going to happen. We all know that this stems back to your annual Christmas parties. Every single year, each of your families tries to outdo the other. It never fails, Wayne somehow gets called in because of it. Now, I'm all about the Christmas spirit—you both should know that better than anyone—which is part of the reason that I've let this go on for as long as I have." Pausing, he sighs. "But this year is when it *stops*. I won't be approving permits for *either* of your parties."

My heart stutters in my chest at what he's saying.

No party?

That's... that's *never* happened in the entire time I've been alive. In all of the years my family has lived in Strawberry Hollow. My family, along with Jackson's, unfortunately, are famous for our annual Christmas parties. The entire town knows this.

"But—" I start, but he shakes his head, silencing me once more. I'm beginning to feel like a chastised child who's gotten punished during this conversation. I understand that what happened was unacceptable, but *this* as a punishment?

"I'm not going to change my mind on this, Emma. If you want to have a party, you'll have it *together* at Town Hall."

My gaze shoots to Jackson's, and I see his jaw working as he clenches his teeth together. Clearly, he's as unhappy about this as I am.

There is absolutely no way that the two of us, much less both of our families, can be in the same room for an extended period of time without someone losing an eyeball.

"Actually, now that I'm saying it out loud, I think that

there is no more perfect plan than this." Mayor Davis smiles, suddenly entirely too happy to be the one to hand down this ridiculous punishment. "Either you have the party *together* at Town Hall, or the general store will go ahead with pressing charges, and this 'accident' will remain on both of your records. *Permanently.*"

"Jed, come on. This isn't happening. Be realistic," Jackson scoffs, his body visibly tensing further as he speaks.

"It is, and it will. This is nonnegotiable. Have the party together or have a permanent record due to your negligence. The choice is yours. I'll expect you to pick a date and get started on the planning, immediately. And one last thing." He glances between us. "Everyone is invited. There's no singling anyone out. The point of this... punishment, per se, is to make both of you and your families understand that Strawberry Hollow values community, and there shouldn't be such bitterness between our residents. We should all come together during this Christmas season and spread joy. It's the reason for the season, after all."

For a moment, everyone is silent. I even almost feel bad for Wayne, who's standing in the back, glancing between the three of us with a somber expression.

Thanks for nothing, Sheriff.

"Throw this party, and bury the hatchet while you're at it. You two caused the damage, so I want the two of you to work together, and I do not want to have to get a call like this again. Understand?"

Obediently, we both nod, and with a smile, he tips his head at us and turns back toward Wayne as if he didn't just flip our entire world upside down on its axis.

Once we've signed the discharge paperwork and have

been officially released, I practically bust through the front doors of the jail, out into the frigid December air, pulling my jacket tighter around me.

I'm so upset, and angry, and just... ready to explode on someone. Particularly the stupidly attractive man on my heels.

"This is *all* your fault!" I grit out as I whip around to face him, my finger pointed in his face. "God, I hate you."

"My fault? How in the hell is this *my* fault? You're the one who decided to fight with me like a petulant child over a fucking Christmas decoration," Jackson retorts, taking a step closer to me. I can feel the frustration radiating off him in thick, pulsating waves.

Good, because I'm frustrated just as much, if not more, than he is. My parents are going to have a colossal meltdown when I break the news that their beloved Christmas party is being... *tainted* by the Pearce family.

That a tradition that has been in our family for generations is now gone, all because of me.

What an absolute mess.

"Clearly, I didn't do this by myself, Pearce. You are just as guilty as I am, and that's exactly why we both just spent the night in jail. I didn't sit there alone."

"Yeah, don't remind me. I just spent the night against my will with Strawberry Hollow's very own ice princess."

My gaze narrows, my chest heaving as we stand toe to toe on the sidewalk outside of the jail.

I heard Mayor Davis loud and clear. I know what the consequences are. I get it.

But... I also don't know how it's physically possible for me to be around this man for longer than thirty seconds without wanting to rip his clothes off while simultaneously wanting to punch him right in his smug face.

It's *not* happening.

There's no way that we can work together.

"This isn't going to work," I mutter defeatedly. "Working with you is *impossible*."

The small space between his dark brows furrows as he shakes his head and leans forward. "Oh... it's happening. I'll be damned if I let you taint my reputation in this town. Looks like we're throwing a party together, *Emmie*."

Joy to the world.

It looks like we're both going to need a Christmas miracle to make it through the next few weeks unscathed.

4 /
jackson

Joy to the world... not.

I need a fucking drink and to forget the past twenty-four hours ever happened. Even if it is barely lunchtime.

I just spent the night in a damn jail cell.

The bell above my head jingles as I push through the old wooden door of the Rusty Rooster, and my best friend, Oliver, greets me with a nod and the biggest shit-eating grin I've ever seen.

"Well, if it isn't the delinquent himself gracing my bar during lunch hour?" He chuckles as he places a glass on the bar top and pours a dark amber whiskey into it before sliding it my way.

Unsurprisingly, the word spread like wildfire, as it usually does. The residents of Strawberry Hollow waste no time when it comes to gossip. That much I know.

The legs of the barstool scrape across the floor as I sit, my fingers folding around the glass and lifting it to my lips. "Ask me how I get into the shit that I do." I sigh, taking a long sip. "This one might actually take the cake though."

Oliver's smirk widens. "Yeah, you two are the talk of the

town, brother. You know how fast news spreads in this town. Already got the down-low from Bree."

I was hoping that I had time to speak with my parents about the events from last night, but I should've known better.

I should've known that everyone would know before lunch. Hell, everyone probably knew before the ink dried from my fingerprinting at the station.

"Haven't I already suffered enough?" I ask, my brows rising in question.

"Nah. I think the suffering has only just begun. But I mean, I guess that depends on who you ask because I, for one, think that Emma Worthington is hot as fuck, and you're an idiot for disliking her."

My gaze narrows. "Yeah, well, she irks my nerves with her holier-than-thou attitude."

I feel my phone going off in my pocket, so I reach down and fish it out of my jeans, glancing at the unknown number on the screen.

A text from an unknown number.

Unknown: Can we please meet to discuss this unfortunate arrangement?

"Speak of the devil," I mutter, raising my gaze to Oliver, who's back to grinning. "Don't say a fucking word."

Me: Sorry, this number is currently disconnected and unavailable to ice princesses. Please try again... *never.*

Emmie: It honestly surprises me how much you continue to prove your immaturity. How does it feel to be over thirty and still a man-child?

Me: Did you text me just to insult me or is there something else I can help you with?

Lifting the glass to my lips, I drain the whiskey, savoring the bite of the liquid as it slides down my throat. Just enough to make it possible to deal with the *ice princess* on the other side of the phone.

Emmie: We have only three weeks to make this disaster of a party happen, and I happen to not like to wait until the last minute to do anything.

Me: What's there to plan? It's a Christmas party. Red, green, a tree, some lights, *lots* of alcohol.

Emmie: I'm not even going to dignify that with an actual response. Tomorrow, 8 am. Hollow Brewhouse. Don't be late.

Me: I'm never late.

Emmie: Something tells me that is not true. Bye, Pearce.

I huff as I set my phone down on the bar and lean back in the barstool.

It's almost Christmas, and even Oliver's bar is decorated for the occasion. There are strings of multicolored Christmas lights draped along the wooden beams above our heads, tinsel lining the bar, and a sad-looking, skinny Christmas tree in the corner by the karaoke stage with Rusty Rooster coasters as ornaments, along with candy canes.

It's about as festive as a bar can get, and while I'm generally excited for the holidays, this year, I haven't felt as much in the spirit. It's always a big deal for our family, so I've been trying not to be a total Scrooge for Ma.

It's just, I'm fucking *swamped* at work, and though I'm thankful as hell to have my business, I haven't had much time to do anything else before I pass out the moment my head hits the pillow.

"How's things at the house coming?" Oliver asks from the other side of the bar.

I shrug. "Slow. Haven't had much time to work on it when I'm constantly working on everyone else's. But I've got a solid crew, and I think I'll be able to delegate a bit more once the holidays have passed."

"Cool. You headin' out?"

"Yeah. Haven't really slept. You know… spent the night in jail," I pull a twenty out of my wallet and put it on the counter. "See you at poker night?"

"Nah, I'm coming to your family dinner this week. I can't wait to hear what your parents have to say about this, and man, I cannot fucking wait to see how this plays out. You two working together and putting this feud to rest? I gotta see it to believe it."

Of course, he can't wait. Dick.

I ARRIVE at the small coffee shop in Town Square approximately five minutes early just to prove a point. Which is almost pointless when I see Emma sitting at a table in the far back, head bent over a spiral-bound notebook.

She lifts her head, a tight smile on her face when she sees me approaching. Her gaze flits to her watch, then back at me as her brow arches. "Wow, four whole minutes early. I guess you proved me wrong."

"Guess I did." I smirk. "I'm going to grab a coffee."

I glance down and see the steaming mug of coffee that's

got what looks like whipped cream, cinnamon, and caramel drizzled over the top.

Of course, she'd drink something... ridiculously frilly when it comes to coffee. Shouldn't expect anything less.

The barista quickly takes my order, and after I've paid, she slides the steaming black coffee across the counter.

Simple. Just the way I like it.

After paying, I walk back to Emma, pulling out the chair and sitting across from her.

"So..." I start.

She rolls her plump lips together before sighing exasperatedly. "Look, I know this isn't ideal, but it's unfortunately what we're working with, and we've got to get along just long enough to get this done. I need you to not be a dick for the next three weeks so we can *actually* pull this off."

I nod. "Fine. You're right. The quicker we can get this over with, the better. What do you need from me?"

As I'm speaking, it feels like I'm being watched, and when I glance around the coffee shop, I see nearly every single pair of eyes on us.

I guess the people in town aren't used to seeing a Worthington having an amicable conversation with a Pearce. Which is fair, seeing as how this is the first time in history anyone from our families has sat down and had coffee together.

Even though this technically isn't by choice.

"Let me guess, literally *everyone* is staring at us?" Emma sighs, refusing to take her eyes off mine.

"Yup."

Only then does she break our stare and drag her gaze out around her, shrinking slightly, as if making herself smaller is somehow going to change the fact that we're the only thing this town has to talk about for the foreseeable future.

"Ignore them. Tell me what you need from me," I say brusquely.

I don't like being the center of attention for any goddamn reason, so the quicker I can get out of this chair, out of this damn building, away from her and the prying eyes of this town, the better.

She nods quickly, reaching behind her to begin pulling things out of her bag.

Pens, highlighters, note cards, a thing of gingerbread-shaped sticky notes, a ruler. And is that a... *poster board*?

What the *fuck* is happening?

"Are we going to class or talking about a Christmas party?" I ask, my brow furrowed.

Emma rolls her eyes and sets out each of the items in a neat row, taking her sweet time.

I can practically hear the whispers of everyone around us getting louder.

Christ.

"Well, unlike you, Pearce, I am extremely detail-oriented and organized. Type A."

"Clearly." Setting my coffee down in front of me, I cross my arms over my chest. "I expected nothing less from you, Emmie."

"*Emma.*"

"Emmie."

She huffs. "Every time I think we might actually have a chance at making this work, you remind me that it's impossible."

I shrug. "A special talent I possess."

Emma rolls her eyes for the second time in two minutes and glances around her at the couple next to us, who are not attempting to hide their gawking and whispering.

"How about we do this somewhere less... crowded?" I ask.

"For once, something we can agree on. Where should we go?" she says, closing the notebook and shoving it and all her supplies into her bag.

"We can go to my house if you're good with it, but I still need to run by a jobsite, so can we do it around six?"

Her blue eyes, which look like the sky after a fresh snow, widen at my suggestion.

Not that I'm particularly excited to have her at my house... but it's quiet, and there won't be prying eyes or people around to gossip about the two of us having to work together.

"Uh, yeah, I guess that could work. Could you text me directions?"

"It's on Maple Hill. Can't miss it," I tell her, standing from my chair.

For a second, she blinks in surprise. "You bought Jacobson's farmhouse?"

I nod. "Yeah. Last winter."

I'm surprised she hasn't heard about it, but I guess she wouldn't be interested in anything that happens with me or my family.

"It's... I mean, it's basically condemned," she says as she finishes placing her supplies back into her bag. "How are you *living* there?"

My chuckle is low as I lean in slightly. "I'm pretty good with my hands."

I don't miss the way her cheeks pink under the fluorescent light of the coffee shop, and I smirk, standing and pushing my chair back under the table.

"See you later, Emmie."

Without another word, I turn on my heel and walk out of the coffee shop to my truck.

Maybe this thing won't be so bad after all, especially if I can make her blush like that again. Only next time... maybe it'll be with my tongue.

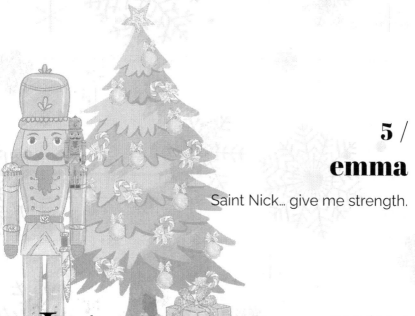

emma

Saint Nick... give me strength.

I can honestly say never in a billion years did I think I would ever be going to Jackson Pearce's *house*. Then again, I never thought I would be able to exist in the same room with him, but somehow, we're both still breathing so far.

"Holy..." I mumble as I pull my Mercedes down the long, winding driveway that leads to his house. Trees hang over the gravel, making it seem that much darker. It's serene and peaceful, completely tucked away from the rest of the world.

Finally, after what feels like a mile, the old white farmhouse comes into view. It's seen much better days, but that makes sense since it spent the better part of twenty years abandoned until apparently Jackson bought it. The paint around the doors and along the front is peeling, the shutters are rustic, and the pillars in the front seem like they could collapse at any moment from their old age.

But despite all of the things wrong with it, there are far more things about this place that are beautiful. The brand-new wraparound porch, the unpainted wood still fresh and new, is breathtaking. Rocking chairs sit out front, along with new windows and a new navy blue front door.

Clearly, Jackson has been renovating, even if it's still a work in progress.

Putting my car in park, I grab my bag from the passenger seat and open the door, stepping out.

A second later, the front door opens and two giant balls of fur come barreling toward me, a blur of fluffy golden hair and floppy ears.

Immediately, a smile spreads on my face as I drop into a squat to get all of the puppy love.

"Oh, hello," I coo, petting each of the heads of two of the cutest Golden Retrievers I've ever seen. "God, you are adorable. Clearly, you two got the looks in the family," I tell them just as Jackson saunters over, his hands pushed deep into the front pockets of his jeans.

"I see you've met Marley and Mo," he says sheepishly. "Calm down, you two heathens."

"They're precious."

He nods. "I rescued them down by the creek. Last December, I stumbled upon them huddled in a bed of wet leaves, tiny little puppies just shivering in the snow. I was surprised they hadn't frozen to death, and when I couldn't find their mama anywhere, I brought them back to the farmhouse, and the rest is history."

Wow, the jerk *does* actually have a heart. That's surprisingly... *adorable.*

Keeping my comment to myself, I nod, plastering on a saccharine smile. "Very noble of you, Jackson Pearce. How many acres do you have here?"

"Twenty. Goes beyond the tree line there and up past

Harrow Creek." Removing his hand from his pocket, he points toward the tree line, where the sun has begun to set in deep orange and purples, bringing the temperature down with it. We haven't had hard snow in the last couple of weeks, so there's only a light dusting along the ground. Enough to cover it, making a fluffy white blanket.

"Let's get inside. You're shivering," he says, noticing a fact that I haven't even yet realized. I was too busy staring at his property and adorable pups.

"Um, yeah, that'd be great."

He turns toward the rustic two-story and calls for the dogs, motioning for me to follow behind him.

I try not to stare at the way the tight denim on his ass is molded to him like a second skin as he walks inside.

Why is it that men who are unreasonably attractive are also equally as annoying?

Maybe it's just a Pearce thing.

I step over the threshold into Jackson's house, my coat pulled tightly around me, and my jaw drops open as I take it all in. While the outside of the house is very clearly still a work in progress, the inside is a completely different story.

Obviously, this is where Jackson started.

The inside is breathtaking, and for the first time, I truly see why everyone in town is obsessed with Pearce Builders.

His craftsmanship is incredible, and the design... it's modern and fresh yet still feels rustic and welcoming.

"Judging a house from the outside, are you?" He chuckles, shutting the door and kicking off his boots in the entryway. "Shouldn't be surprised, Emmie."

Rolling my eyes, I do the same. As I'm shrugging out of

my jacket, he takes it from me, surprising me, and hangs it on the coat rack.

"I am not judging the house. I... I just wasn't expecting it to be so beautiful. I mean, the house sat abandoned for so long the entire town was convinced that it would have to be condemned. Clearly, that's not true. You've put a lot of work into it."

He leads me into the open-floor-plan living room, where there's a comfortable cream couch and a massive TV mounted on the wall. "Did it kill you to give me that compliment? I feel like it had to have hurt."

The smile on his lips is teasing, and I scowl, narrowing my eyes. "Enjoy it because it'll never happen again."

I set my bag down on the coffee table and then do a slow one-eighty, taking in the rest of his house, the dark wood floor and black iron light fixtures.

"Do you care if I set my stuff up here, or would you prefer somewhere else?"

He shrugs, nodding toward the dark wooden coffee table. "Have at it. Mo and Marley will probably want all the attention if you're on the floor though."

"No complaints from me—they're so cute. Thanks."

Dragging my gaze from his, I rummage through my bag and pull out all of my supplies: notebook, calendar, stickies, highlighters, colored pens. My mood board. Everything I need to make sure this goes smoothly, as organized as humanly possible.

It's going to be hard enough for the two of us to work together without both of us losing our minds, and even harder if I don't stay on top of everything.

Plus, it helps me feel... in control of a situation when I'm prepared. I need everything to go exactly as planned, and the only way to do that is to plan.

What's that saying... fail to plan, plan to fail?

Jackson disappears into the kitchen, then returns with two amber bottles of beer in his hand. "Beer? I know it's probably not fancy enough for you, but it's all I've got. Not a red wine kinda guy." He extends it toward me.

Glaring at him, I take the bottle from his hand. "Now who's judging who? I happen to *love* beer. I drink it all the time. I'm a real beer connoisseur."

Amusement flickers in his eyes as I take a hefty sip, never breaking our stare.

The second the bitter liquid hits my taste buds, I immediately regret my decision.

God, it takes like... carbonated muddy water, except even worse, and I don't know how that's possible. Trying to keep a straight face, I swallow the mouthful and grimace. "*Delicious.* Thank you."

He tosses his head back, a deep, low rumble erupting from his chest. "God, you're a shit liar, Emmie. The look on your face was priceless."

I ignore him entirely, taking a seat between his couch and the coffee table and setting the beer on the table. "Do you have a coaster?"

"Do I *look* like the kind of guy who has a coaster?"

Sighing, I open the notebook and uncap my pen as he sits on the floor next to me, bringing his beer to his lips.

Even though it tastes horrible, I continue to sip my beer, if only to prove a point that I'm not "too good" for beer. For someone who doesn't know me at all, he sure does have a lot of preconceived notions about who I am. Although, I guess that's not entirely fair because I've done the same to him.

"Okay, so I think we should get started."

He nods. "Have at it, Emmie."

My gaze narrows as I take another hefty sip of my beer, and for a second, I don't bother to hide the slow perusal as I drink him in. Maybe it's the alcohol or that I've barely eaten all day... or *maybe* it's that it's been a long time since I've been this close to Jackson Pearce. The jail cell didn't count—I was in distress and trying to focus on getting free again.

It's at this moment that I realize being this close to Jackson Pearce is *dangerous*.

It's his whiskey-brown eyes, the gold flecks of honey that swirl around his irises. Thick, dark lashes frame them, a shade darker than the stubble on his chin that he hasn't bothered to shave. I'm usually more of a clean-cut, suit-and-tie kind of girl, but there's something deliciously enticing about him. Something dangerous and rough. Something I find myself *wanting*.

His tawny, chestnut hair is perpetually disheveled, falling in his face as he leans back against the couch, bringing the bottle to his lips. The strong column of his throat bobs as he swallows the beer down, and I clench my thighs together when I feel a throb.

Okay, maybe this beer is going to my head. Or maybe it's the fact that he rescues freaking puppies from the cold or the fact that he sees the beauty in a house that everyone else was so quick to condemn. I mean... maybe there's more to Jackson Pearce than I ever realized because I was too blinded by what I thought I knew?

No. It's *definitely* the beer. *Only* the beer.

That's exactly what's happening right now.

The alcohol is making my brain fuzzy, making it impossible to think clear, rational thoughts because they're clouded by Jackson Pearce.

That's why I'm looking at his forearms like they're my own special version of porn, the tanned muscles rippling as he moves the beer back down to rest on his denim-clad thigh.

"Emma?" His voice breaks through my thoughts, and I feel my cheeks heat, a furious blush spreading in its wake.

Not only am I delusionally picturing Jackson naked, but I'm doing it while sitting *right* next to him. I can feel the heat of his body next to mine, smell the fresh, woodsy scent of his shampoo.

"So." I clear my throat, dragging my gaze back to the notebook in front of me as I start writing. "I was thinking that we start at Town Hall? We need to access the building, take some measurements, see what we're really working with. I actually haven't been in Town Hall in years, so I need to see what exactly I'm up against."

"Sure. Whatever you think." My gaze drags to his, and I linger on the fullness of his lips before shaking my head and pulling my eyes back to the notebook in front of me.

I'll start with a checklist. That always keeps all of the little boxes in my head straight. Organized.

"Okay, perfect. So, I was thinking maybe a standard five-course dinner? Black-and-white cocktail attire. Make it a fancy affair an—"

"Woah, woah, woah." He stops me, shaking his head. "Emmie, hate to disappoint you, but we are *not* having a fucking fancy black-tie party for this. Half the people in this town don't even own the attire for that."

I scoff. "And when you say half the people, you're really referring to the Pearces, correct?"

"No, I'm referring to *Strawberry Hollow*. You know, since the entire town is supposed to be invited. Shit, you know what? I'm gonna need another beer for this." Without another word, he stands from the floor and disappears into the kitchen, returning with two more bottles. In my distraction of accidentally eye-fucking my enemy, I guess I finished the beer he gave me.

The taste kind of *does* grow on you...

He extends the beer to me, sans the top, and sits down next to me, this time angling his body to face me.

"Listen, I know that your family has traditions, and you want this to be a fancy affair, but you also have to consider that *my* family has traditions. And if we're going to do this *together*, we're going to have to work together, *Snowflake*. Even if this is the last thing either of us wants to be doing."

Damn him.

He's right...

"Fine. We can learn to... *compromise*. But you can't shoot an idea down as soon as I suggest it, Pearce. That's only fair."

He holds his hands up in surrender. "Fine, but the same goes for you. Works both ways."

I nod, avoiding his gaze. I'm seriously on the fence about asking him if there's an aphrodisiac or something in this beer because I am increasingly *horny*.

For... Jackson Pearce.

6 /
jackson

HO.... me for the holidays.

I can *almost* stand Emma like this. Relaxed, less uptight, less *mouthy*. Every single time she opens her mouth to be a little brat, I want to put her on her knees and fill it.

I can't fucking help it, and sitting this close to her, the flames crackling in the fireplace, the room dimly lit, I'm focusing on all of the wrong things. Things I know I shouldn't be concentrating on, yet the task feels impossible.

"Okay, so that's a start. A plan. We meet at Town Hall, measure the area, see what we're working with for the party space. That's a veto on the five-course meal. Got it." As she speaks, she's checking things off her to-do list. Perfect little check marks, not that I expected anything less. "Now, we *have* to decide on a theme so we can figure out the decorations, food, and entertainment in more detail," she says, setting her sparkly pen down to grab her beer and take a long sip.

That's how we spend the next thirty minutes, going over this "plan" of hers, occasionally taking jabs at each other when the opportunity presents itself, and somehow ending up so close that we're brushing against each other with every small movement.

"God, there are so many fucking sticky notes I can't even keep up at this point." I groan, swiping one of the ginger-bread notes off the table. "And this? An *ice sculpture*? No, Emmie. Abso-fucking-lutely not."

She scoffs, snatching the sticky note back out of my hand with an unladylike snort. "You're impossible, you do realize that, right? An ice sculpture is classy, and do not touch my sticky notes, please—they are organized just the way I need them to be."

I smirk, leaning over her with my gaze locked on hers.

I pluck another from the table and hold it between my forefingers. We're so close now that I can feel her breath fanning my lips. "*Whoops.*"

Her gaze narrows as her brow arches, and my smirk widens when she tries to snatch it from my hand. I hold it high above her head... *just* out of reach.

We're in a silent standoff, one that I'm taking far too much pleasure in.

I couldn't tell you which one of us moved first, but all of a sudden, we're on each other, my hands lacing into her silky hair as I yank her the rest of the distance toward me, sealing my lips over hers and tasting the beer on her tongue. Her hands slide along the nape of my neck, and then she's scram-bling into my lap, seated directly on my already aching cock while whimpering against my lips.

Fuck, as much as I pretend to hate this girl, I *want* her. Badly.

I want to be the one that strips away all of the hard, prim

exterior, leaving her soft and pliable beneath my calloused hands.

My fingers ghost along the sliver of skin that peeks out from her sweater, which has risen, a shiver sliding down her spine when I do. For someone who spends so much time pretending to hate *me*, she's so fucking responsive to my touch.

Her hips circle on my lap as her nails bite into my scalp, trying to drag me even closer against her, her lips battling with mine in a kiss that I feel in every single nerve ending of my body. I'm trying to be the gentleman she seems to expect me to be, but that's not who I am.

There is nothing gentlemanly about the way I want to fuck her. Nothing gentlemanly about the things I want to do to her.

To take off her clothes, worship her body with my tongue, and show her just how much of a brat she is with my handprints blooming bright red on her ass.

Sliding my hands higher along her back, I press her against me, rocking her hips over my cock until we're both panting and breathless. A tangle of tongue and teeth. It's frantic, and there's nothing elegant about it, unlike everything I've ever known Emma Worthington to be.

Her tongue drags along my lower lip before she captures it between her teeth and tugs at the same time her fingers snake beneath the fabric of my shirt, brushing along the planes of my stomach. The muscles contract beneath her touch, and I'm two seconds from tearing what I'm sure is something ridiculously expensive off her body and fucking her right here on this floor.

When my fingers brush along the lacy strap of her bra, she

pulls back and stares at me through heavy-lidded, desire-filled eyes framed by thick, dark lashes.

Staring at each other, panting hard, I can practically see the thoughts running through her mind.

"Shit. What are we doing? We shouldn't be doing this." She tries to crawl off my lap, but I palm her ass, rocking into her slightly, and her head drops back with a moan, her fingers clawing into my stomach. Leaning forward, I capture her lips again, delving into her mouth and showing her exactly why we *should* be doing this.

Fuck the feud, fuck the fact that we're supposed to hate each other, fuck everything that isn't right here, right now. I've always been attracted to her, even if she drives me insane like no other, but being forced together these last two days has made me want her that much more. This is not something that's going to go away, so fuck it.

We'll worry about the aftermath later.

Tearing my lips from hers, I trail them lower along her jaw to her neck, where I suck at the sensitive spot below her ear. "This is exactly why we *should*, Snowflake."

She moans when I drag my teeth along her skin, nipping while she squirms.

"B-but we hate each other," she pants, threading her hands in my hair again and tugging. *Hard.*

Fuck yes, I knew there was more to this girl, hiding under her holier-than-thou attitude.

"Never said I hated you. In fact..." I slide my hands under her sweater, dragging my palms along her stomach as I inch the soft fabric up, higher and higher, exposing the light pink lace of her bra and the swell of her tits. There's a tiny gold heart dangling from the center clasp of the bra. "I happen to fucking *love* these."

I cup them in my palms, squeezing and pushing them together as my thumb brushes along the hard pebble of her nipple.

"We... shouldn't." She can barely get the words out over her pants as I drag my tongue along the edge of the lace. "We..." Even as she's protesting, she's grinding on my cock.

Pulling back, I gaze at her. "How about we worry about what we shouldn't be doing later? Clearly, we're attracted to each other, and this feels good. We're adults, Emma."

Her breath hitches when I use her name instead of the many nicknames I use just to annoy her.

"One night. That's all I want."

She blinks back at me, hesitation flickering in her gaze, but ultimately nods. "*One* night. And we never speak of it again. We pretend it *never* happened."

It sounds like she's trying to convince herself, but I just shrug, my lip quirking up. "Sure, Snowflake. We can go back to pretending we hate each other... *tomorrow*."

Nodding again, she sits back slightly, pulling down her sweater, but I reach up to stop her.

"Don't hide from me." Leaning forward, I close my lips around the tight peak hidden beneath pale pink lace. The color complements her pale, creamy skin, and it makes me want to leave marks all over her, claiming her. A little reminder that after tonight, no one will be able to make her feel the way I did, even if she wants to go back to pretending once tonight is over.

"Don't boss me ar—" I slam my lips on hers, silencing her,

our tongues thrashing together in a punishing kiss, one that erases all the sass from her bratty little mouth.

Fuck, I want to spank it right out of her, leave marks on her delectable ass. My hands travel down to squeeze it as I lift us from the floor easily and walk over to the plush rug in front of the crackling fire. Close enough to feel the heat but far enough back that it's not uncomfortable.

Her blonde hair is spread out beneath her, her lips red and swollen from our kisses, and her cheeks flushed a delicious pink.

She looks fucking beautiful.

I don't give her a second to overthink or to question. I simply part her thighs and plant myself between them, yanking at her sweater until it's over her head and tossed to the side.

Leaning forward, I press my lips softly against the curve of her cleavage while her fingers lace into the hair at my nape, pushing me against her chest as a needy sound escapes her lips.

A sound that I've committed to memory and plan to hear over and over again tonight.

My fingers dip beneath the lace cups, pulling one down to reveal a rosy pink nipple that is only a shade darker than her lips. I bring my lips to it, dragging my teeth along the peak before sucking it into my mouth and then letting go with a pop.

"Jackson..." she pants, pulling my head back when I lift up, my eyes roaming her chest. "*Please.*"

Never in my life did I think I'd have Emma Worthington begging me for anything, let alone beneath me.

I slide my hand beneath her and unclasp her bra, the

straps falling loosely down her arms as I pull it off, leaving her naked from the waist up.

For a second, I'm frozen at the sight.

Her spread out in front of me, blonde hair fanned out around her like a halo glowing from the flames of the fire, pale pink nipples hardened into tight little peaks that are begging to be sucked and bitten. She's aching for my cock. For my tongue on her.

There are only a few things in life that I believe would truly bring me to my knees, and I know without a doubt that this is one of them.

Emma Worthington is one of them.

Her hands reach for me, hurrying me along, and I shake my head. "If I've only got one night with you, Emma, I'm taking every fucking second of it," I say, tracing my tongue along her nipple. "*Don't* rush me. Let me look at you." My voice is hoarse with need, and I don't miss the way she squirms beneath me when I speak.

My tongue dips to the hollow of her chest between her tits, trailing lower and lower in a path to her navel, where I dip it inside before tracing the skin above her waistband.

I quickly pop the button of her pants free, and when she shimmies them down her hips, I toss them to the side, leaving her in nothing but pale pink lace with a damp spot on the front.

Fuck, I want to taste her. I want her to soak my face until I'm drenched in her.

My tongue sweeps across the lace, and she gasps as I tear it from her body in a single rough pull.

"Jackson!" she mumbles in a breathless protest. "Those were *expensive*."

"Don't care. Take my card and buy a thousand fucking pairs," I grunt in response, my eyes flicking to her bare pussy just inches from my face. She's soaked, and I can fucking smell her arousal.

In the dim light of the fire, she's glistening as I use my fingers to spread her open wide, my eyes raking over her perfect pussy.

"Goddamn," I mutter, unable to stop myself from flattening my tongue and dragging it through her wetness. I reach down, palming my cock, which is now impossibly fucking hard and seeping just from the taste of her.

Her hands fly to my hair, tugging at the strands as a soft cry tumbles from her lips.

She tastes so sweet I want to stay here for the rest of the night, licking her clit, fucking her with my tongue until she's sated and exhausted from all of the times she comes. But with only one night, I have to use my time wisely.

I flick her clit, swirling my tongue around the bud once, and then again before sucking it into my mouth. Hard.

Her back bows from the rug, her hips bucking against my mouth as I slide a finger inside of her, hooking it up to hit the spot that has her writhing. She's tight and warm, clenching around my fingers as I fuck her.

The sound of me eating her pussy like a starved man, combined with the sloppy sounds of her pussy taking my fingers, fills the room. It's dirty and unhinged, but fuck, that's exactly how I feel about her right now.

That's exactly what *this* is.

"Oh God, Jackson..." she pants, and my cock pulses at how fucking good it sounds to hear my name on her lips. For her to say my name in pleasure instead of with animosity.

I want to hear it over and fucking over again, echoing on the walls of my house as I sink my cock into her and fuck the shit out of her.

I've barely started, and she's already close, her walls tightening around my fingers.

"Come, Emma. On my tongue," I command, loving the way she tugs harder on my hair when I suck her clit into my mouth, then add another finger inside of her, stroking her G-spot. "Soak my face, Snowflake."

The nickname that she hates so much is what finally sends her over the edge, that and the bite to her thigh that has her legs snapping closed around my head. Her back arches, a flood of wetness coating my tongue.

I lap at her pussy as she writhes, the orgasm rocking through her, making her entire body tense until she's sensitive and pushing me away.

With one last gentle press of my lips to her clit, I climb up her body, caging her in with a smug grin on my lips. I bring my fingers to my mouth, holding her gaze as I suck them clean, savoring the taste of her. "Your pussy sure doesn't hate me, Emmie, because you just came all over my face."

"Don't say another word," she says, leveling her gaze on me. "Not a single word, Pearce."

My brow arches. "Back to last names, are we?"

Even in the dim light of the fire, I can see her cheeks are flushed, and her lips are swollen from my kisses. The sight of her freshly orgasmed is *almost* as sexy as the creamy skin of her inner thighs, which are now scratched and red from my beard brushing against them as I ate her pussy. As she practically rode my face.

It causes something primal to stir inside of me, an unfamiliar feeling of possessiveness rising to the surface. I want to mark her everywhere. Not just her thighs.

Her ass, her pussy. I want to paint her with my cum.

I feel her hand brush along my jean-clad cock, and I hiss in response, my gaze lingering on hers.

"One night," she repeats our words from earlier, squeezing my length through the thick fabric. She toys with the button, popping it free, then lowering my zipper slowly.

Leaning forward, I capture her lips, swallowing her whimper as we work together to unbutton my shirt. When it takes longer than anticipated, she lets out a frustrated huff against my mouth.

I chuckle, then reach behind me and pull it off at the neck. Before I can even toss it to the side, her hands are on me, roaming over the expanse of my chest, to my abs, and lower to where my pants hang open.

"God, of course you'd be built like some... *Greek god.*" It sounds like a compliment, but I'm pretty sure she means it as an insult.

"What were you expecting, Snowflake?" I murmur, pushing the jeans down my hips until they're off and out of the way.

She rolls her lips between her teeth before speaking. "Not this."

"A shame." I smirk, hovering back over her. "Sorry to exceed your expectations."

My fingers trail along her outer thigh, and she shivers in response. All that's left between us is the thin fabric of my boxer briefs, and I couldn't hide my stiff, aching cock if I fucking tried. Not with how badly I want to fuck her, how badly I want to see her break apart beneath me.

Her fingers dip into the waistband of my boxer briefs, and she tugs at them until they're over my hips so the head of my cock peeks from the top, a bead of precum seeping from the slit.

I watch as her expression turns hungry, her eyes becoming hazy and unfocused as she swallows thickly. Then she surprises me by pulling me toward her, moving her lips over mine, teasing the seam of my mouth until I open and she's sucking on my tongue like she's as desperate as I am.

I quickly push my boxers the rest of the way down, my cock bobbing free against my stomach, and she pulls back, her gaze dropping between us.

"Jesus," she murmurs as she rises from the floor and then pushes me onto the rug and straddles me. "I want you."

"Feeling's mutual," I muse.

She moves over me until my cock brushes against her warm, soaked center, and we both groan in unison at the sensation. Placing her hands on my chest, she squirms in my lap, slicking my cock with her wetness.

I suck in a breath as her nails bite into my skin, her hips writhing over my cock, a soft moan leaving her lips each time the head of my cock brushes her throbbing clit.

"You want to use me to come, Snowflake?"

She nods, still circling her hips and dragging her clit along my cock. Judging by how flushed her cheeks are, the way her lips are parted, and her eyes squeezed tightly shut, she's already close again.

As badly as I want to be inside her, I want to watch her bring *herself* to orgasm, wildly gliding her pussy on my dick. Something that will undoubtedly live in my head rent fucking free.

My hands fly to her hips, and I guide her on my cock, licking my lips as I watch her drop her head back. She brings her hand to her nipple, rolling it between her fingers and giving it a rough yank. A second later, she's shattering, her legs shaking as she comes. I can feel the gush of liquid on my cock, and my balls fucking ache to release inside of her. She's still trembling from her orgasm as I line my cock up with her entrance and slowly sink her down on me an inch.

"Fuck. Emma, a condom."

We both freeze. I can't believe I got so caught up in the moment I didn't even pause to think about it. That's *never* happened before.

"I'm on birth control, and I was just tested. I want to feel you bare," she breathes, sinking down an inch further. "If… you want." She's sucking her lip into her mouth, a wanton look in her eyes, and we both know that there's no stopping this.

There's nothing in this fucking world I want more than pumping her full of my cum, to feel her wet pussy clamping down on my cock as she comes.

"Same," I grunt and grab her hips, thrusting into her and burying myself to the hilt all at once.

"God… Jackson, I'm so full," she pants, rocking her hips back and forth so her clit brushes against the base of me. "I've never felt so… stretched."

She's going to make me come in thirty goddamn seconds if she keeps talking like this. I've never been inside a woman bare. It's taking every bit of self-restraint I have not to rut into her and pump her so full of cum that she'll think of me for days after. My muscles shake with the strain to hold myself back.

"Stop moving," I groan. "Give me a second, woman."

She giggles, a sound I never thought I'd hear from Emma. It makes sense that it's at my expense, and thankfully, she complies, holding still briefly.

I feel her clench around me, her gaze darkening to make the irises of her blue eyes look like the deepest depths of the ocean.

"You're definitely on the naughty list," I tease, flipping us over to where her back hits the soft fur of the rug, my cock still buried inside of her.

I pull her leg higher up on my side, setting the arch of her foot along my shoulder so I can fuck her even deeper. She sighs a breathy whimper as my hips flex.

"I need you to stop talking and *fuck me*, Jackson Pearce."

My brow arches. Most of the time, she drives me up a fucking wall, but damn, I think I actually love that mouth. I love how feisty she is. A fucking spitfire, never taking any shit from anyone.

It's the things that I *didn't* know about Emma that I'm committing to memory right now. The way she sounds as she comes, the way we somehow fit perfectly together even though we've been taught to hate each other for our entire lives. How right she feels on my dick.

Her legs rest on my shoulders, and I feel the tremor in them when I thrust my hips deeper, bottoming out inside of her. With every thrust, her tits shake, and she moves further up on the rug.

There's nothing gentle or romantic about what's happening between us.

It's raw, lust-filled fucking, both of us giving in to our bodies' desire for each other. Tomorrow, we'll worry about the consequences, but tonight, losing myself in her is the only place I want to be.

My gaze drops to where I'm fucking her, and I spread her open further so I can better watch my cock slide into her. It's the hottest thing I've ever seen. Watching her stretch to take all of me, her pussy pink and puffy from my cock pounding inside of her.

I feel her tightening around me and the tingling in the base of my spine intensifying, pushing me closer to the edge.

I withdraw and surge forward forcefully, my thrusts turning more erratic and wild, and she whimpers beneath me. Leaning down, I capture the taut peak of her nipple between my teeth to bite as I drop my fingers down to her clit, circling in sync with my thrusts.

"Come, Emma," I rasp against her nipple, my other hand fisting the soft curve of her hip as my balls begin to draw up, ready to explode.

"I- I..." she pants.

I pinch her clit between my fingers, and her orgasm sweeps through her violently, her back bowing and her legs clamping around my hips as she writhes.

A second later, I follow, arousal snaking down my spine. I rock my hips into her slower, delving deep as I let go, coming inside of her in hot spurts. A deep groan sounds from my chest, and my hands grasp tightly on to her waist as the aftershocks of her orgasm rock through her.

"Holy shit," she mumbles, glancing up at me with darkened pupils and flushed cheeks.

This was dirty, and rough, and hot as fuck.

And suddenly, I find myself wishing it was for more than the one night we promised.

7 /
emma

Mistle-No

I feel like I've got a neon sign over my head that says, "I had the best sex of my life with a man I sometimes want to murder," and it's following me around everywhere I go. And by sometimes, I mean all of the time that he isn't giving me orgasms.

Logically, I know that's not true, but it seems like ever since the night that we shall not discuss, the entire town has been whispering and following me with their eyes even more than usual.

"You're being paranoid, Emma. Chill," I mutter to myself, closing my eyes and counting to ten, then exhaling a steady breath.

"What was that, darling?"

My eyes fly open, and I see my mother standing in the kitchen, her brow furrowed in question, which is saying a lot considering the amount of money she spends each month on Botox.

I clear my throat and shake my head, pasting on a smile. "Nothing, I was just going over my to-do list in my head. I just wanted to sit with you really quick and go over a few things."

A few things being that I might actually be the worst Worthington in the history of my entire bloodline. I nervously chew my lip as she nods and gestures to the grand dining room table. As always, it's set to perfection.

I wouldn't expect anything less from Amelia Worthington. Everything in our household has *always* been proper and organized, or my mother would lose her mind, and nobody wanted that. I grew up realizing from a very early age that my mother expected the very same perfection out of me, and somewhere along the way, the pressure to be what she expected me to be began to feel... suffocating.

More so now than ever. I hated to disappoint her, even as an adult.

"Well, sit down, Emma, you're making me nervous," she says from the opposite chair.

"Sorry, I'm feeling a bit, uh, distracted today." I pull out the chair and smooth the back of my skirt before taking a seat. Her gaze is trained on me as I sit there in silence.

I don't know the right way to come out and say it, so I'm just going to say it and get it over with.

"There was a little... altercation a few days ago. I know you were out of town for the work trip with Dad, and I wanted to be the first one to tell you. "

Her eyebrows rise slightly, causing her brows to reach the blonde wisps of her bangs. She's wearing her hair half up and half down today, secured tightly with a Chanel clip that's almost the same shade as the red on her lips. Her signature color.

She's always said that it's the perfect shade to match the

bloodred ruby earrings my father gifted her on their first wedding anniversary. Her makeup is flawless and her clothing classy yet effortlessly casual.

My mother has always been the face of the ladies society in Strawberry Hollow. A perfect Worthington woman, which means that she has always set the bar high.

"What kind of altercation?" she asks, her expression scandalized.

"I ran into Jackson Pearce at the general store, and we had a small... disagreement. It was honestly so silly, and I realize that now, but as you know, the Pearce family has the uncanny ability to push you like no other. I didn't realize in my argument with him how close I was to the glass ornament display, and when I stepped back... it fell over and shattered."

My mother gasps, covering her mouth. "Oh, Emma!"

"Obviously, it was an accident. A terrible accident, and to make a very long, ridiculously silly story short, there were consequences. Consequences I was totally prepared to handle, but unfortunately, Mayor Davis says that neither the Pearce family nor the Worthingtons can have a Christmas party... unless it's at Town Hall. Together."

I've never seen my mother go as pale as she does when she hears the news. For a second, she's frozen in shock, her perfect face unmoving.

"I know it's not the best-case scenario, but I think that it will be o—"

"Emma." She finally speaks, her voice rising with every word. "Do you mean to say that we have to be around the... Pearce family. To have our annual Christmas party... *together*?"

I nod, biting my lip, unsure if the question is actually one she wants me to answer or if she's just in shock.

She stands abruptly, the sound of her heels clicking against the marble tile as she paces the dining room. It's rare to see her so... *frazzled*. My mother is always the picture of calm and put together. Seeing her this way is slightly unnerving.

"This might actually be what causes your father to have a heart attack. Don't you remember last year? My goodness, it took him an entire week to calm down after that whole debacle. Flipping all of our outdoor decorations upside down. The nerve! To come onto our property and vandalize it in such a way." She mumbles, her fingers massaging her temples, still pacing. "And now you're saying we have to host the party with the very family that has tried to disrupt our tradition for years? This is not good, Emma, not good at all."

I nod sheepishly, even though I'm not surprised by her reaction.

Finally, she pauses in front of me, composing herself. She raises her chin slightly as if this is only a small blip in her day.

"And you're *absolutely sure* that there is no other way around this... situation?"

"Well, it's either this or I'll have a criminal record."

The sound that leaves her mouth is part gasp, part pained whimper, and it causes me to shrink back slightly in my chair. I *hate* disappointing my family in any way, and I can practically feel it rolling off her in waves.

"Out of the question. Not even in the *realm* of possibility." Blowing out an exasperated breath that moves the wisps of her bangs, she continues. "But it seems like there is not another option, is there? As unfortunate as it is, you and...

Mr. Pearce will have to work together to make this happen, Emma. Not only to keep your record and your namesake clean but because we will not have the Worthington name attached to just any basic party. We have a reputation to uphold in this community. You know how important this party is to the Worthingtons. It's *our* family's tradition. Worthingtons have been hosting the town Christmas party ever since our town was founded, when our ancestors first settled in Strawberry Hollow."

"I know, Mom. Which is why I already have a plan and have been keeping on top of everything to make sure there aren't any issues along the way. Everything will go flawlessly. We simply spend a few hours mingling among them and the rest of the town, and it'll be over before we know it. Easy. But I'll make sure the party is still amazing, one worthy of the Worthington name. Then next year, we'll go back to normal." I glance down at the watch on my wrist and back to her. "I'm due at Town Hall in the next hour to meet Jackson Pearce."

Mom nods, regaining her mask of composure that she momentarily let slip. "Very well. Let me worry about telling your father. You just make sure that you handle this and uphold the Worthington reputation. Let me make you some tea before you get on the road."

And just like that, doing what she absolutely does best, she goes back to pretending that everything is perfect and nothing is amiss.

I'm the one who got locked up and then accidentally slept with the enemy, and now there's no getting out of being around him until this party is over.

PARKING my Mercedes in the only other unoccupied parking space in front of Town Hall, I grab my bag and step out onto the sidewalk as I eye Jackson's old, rusty truck parked in front.

It looks like one strong gust of wind could have it in heaps of metal on the ground. The paint is chipping, and the tailgate is rusted where the letters CHEVROLET are on the back.

"Judging my truck like you judged my house, Emmie?" A deep voice comes from right beside me, causing me to startle and drop my bag onto the concrete, its contents scattering all over the ground.

Jesus, I almost just had a heart attack.

"Damn, you're jumpy today. Thinking of anything in particular? Anyone?" I can see the cocky grin on his face, and if he wasn't so damn infuriating, I might want to kiss him. *Again.*

Which is definitely out of the question. It was a one-and-done kind of thing.

"Well, that's generally what happens when you sneak up on an unsuspecting woman." Bending, I start to gather everything and shove it back into my bag as he joins me to help. He smells just like he did the other night, crisp and clean, masculine. The kind of smell that you pick in a candle store that reminds you of the dreamiest man.

Which is seriously not helping the fact that I am supposed to be hating him again, not wanting to take him for a ride like Santa's sleigh.

"Emmie?" he asks, his voice low as he squats in front of me.

"What?"

Chuckling, he shakes his head. "I called your name a few times. I asked if you were okay. You seem... off today."

Swiping the rest of my stuff into my bag, I plaster on a cool smile, even though I'm feeling anything but right now. I'm extremely flustered and now beginning to doubt whether I will somehow be able to pull this off at all. I can't even *look* at him without remembering him between my thighs, his beard brushing against the sensitive skin of my legs as he ate me like a starving man. Or how he felt buried deep inside me, my toes curling on his shoulders.

I stand, brushing off my suede pencil skirt, and hold my bag against my chest. "Never better. Ready?"

He eyes me for a moment before shrugging, and I give myself just twenty seconds of checking him out before we walk into Town Hall. Today, he's wearing a pair of dark jeans, old, scuffed work boots, and a dark green Henley that is practically molded to the muscles of his biceps.

"After you, Snowflake," he murmurs when he catches me looking at him, his dark amber eyes smoldering in the way only they can.

Ignoring the nickname, I brush past him toward Town Hall and pull open the heavy front door, letting myself inside.

My first thought is how dark it is, with little to no natural light, and it smells like stale, old *mothballs*. It's probably been a year since Town Hall has been used, judging by the amount of dust coating every surface.

My nose scrunches at the sight. God, I have *so* much work cut out for me.

"Fuck yeah. There's a bar!" Jackson says excitedly.

Of course, the primary thing he's worried about is alcohol. Not the place being outdated, dirty, and barely inhabitable.

Why am I not surprised?

"Can you channel your excitement for drinking into something productive like... helping me measure or, I don't know... figuring out how to let this place air out?"

Jackson walks over, crossing his arms over his chest. "There's nothing wrong with this place, Emmie. Very... *vintage*. Little spit and shine, and she'll be good as new."

"Please never say that. Ever again."

"Why? Making you think about the other night?" He smirks.

Saint Nick help me, but I am. Apparently, my vagina is a ho ho ho for this man, which is very, *very* problematic.

I close the distance between us in two short strides. "I thought we agreed that we would never, ever, under any circumstance bring that night up again?"

He shrugs. "Did we?"

"You're infuriating. Has anyone ever told you how absolutely infuriating you are?" I retort, rolling my eyes. "Look, clearly, that was a mistake. One we agreed we would never bring up again, so please, can we... not? This is already complicated enough as it is, and we don't even like each other, Jackson."

"I mean, you liked when I had my coc—" Reaching out, I slap my hand over his mouth to silence him, feeling his lips tugging up beneath my fingers.

Asshole.

"Don't. Seriously, Jackson, this is truly *never* going to work if we don't both act like adults and realize that it was an error in judgment and move on. We fucked. It happened, and now we're moving past it like it never happened."

I remove my hand from his mouth, and only then do I notice that his whiskey-colored eyes have darkened. He steps forward until the tips of his dirty boots touch my stiletto boots. "Don't worry, Snowflake. You'll be begging me for my cock again soon."

My jaw drops in shock. Excuse me? That… He's…

Before I can even form a response to that, he's halfway across the room, pulling a measuring tape out of the back pocket of his sinfully tight, faded jeans.

I don't let my gaze linger and instead stride over to him. "So you're just going to measure… What, exactly?"

"Clearly, we're not getting anywhere standing around, talking about things that don't matter, right?" His brows rise as if repeating my own words back to me is going to win this argument. "Might as well make good use of the time. What do you need from me?"

Sighing, I walk back over to my bag and pull out my notebook and pen, opening it to the last page I took notes on before… that night happened.

"Uh… Theme. You said you're against a black-tie cocktail affair, but we have to meet in the middle somewhere. Can we at least have a sit-down, formal dinner? If not, I worry my parents might not even come to the damn party, and it's important to them, okay? I know you probably don't care, but this party is a centuries-old tradition for my family."

"Sure, but I'm not using five forks, and I'm definitely not eating some crazy shit like caviar. How about a sit-down dinner with *regular* Christmas food? Turkey? Roast? Something everyone likes?"

I nod, brushing my hair out of my face as I write it down in my notebook. "Fine. Champagne? Beer?"

Even though the thought of drinking another beer makes me want to gag, I know we should have a variety for everyone.

"Definitely. Maybe some seltzers? BYOB or a paid bar?"

"BYOB? Oh no. A paid bar," I say, jotting it down. "What about hiring someone to play piano?"

Jackson's brows tug together in obvious distaste as he sighs. "Emmie, listen, I understand that you want this to be something fancy, and that's what your family has always done. I get it. I do, I *really* do. But I also need you to understand that my family parties... aren't like that. We've got to meet somewhere in the middle," he says, parroting back my earlier words. "No piano, but what about a band? Something festive and fun and not so... cold? No offense."

I try not to take offense at that as I scribble it down. "Okay, we can decide on which band later, but the rest sounds okay. For an overall theme, what about... a winter wonderland? We can dress that theme up or down?"

He nods. "Don't really care about the decorations, Snowflake."

Thank God. I can't imagine fighting with him over the color of the decorations.

"Okay, well, I was thinking maybe some real fir garland here? And a few candles on each table to set the tone. Even just a few pieces here and there can make it look classy and elegant. Could you, uh... measure the wall right there?"

He nods, then disappears through the door leading to the back of Town Hall, returning a few moments later with a rickety ladder that's missing the bottom rung.

"Uh, are you *sure* you should be climbing on that? It looks like it's going to fall apart the moment you step foot on it." He shoots me a look that says he's got it covered, so I raise my hands in surrender and go back to writing in my notebook.

I feel slightly better now that we've gotten some of the major things nailed down, and much easier than I anticipated. But there's still so much to do and so little time.

"Jackson, I—" Just as I call his name, he looks back at me, and the metal of the decrepit ladder groans under his weight, then gives out, sending him barreling backward. I run over like I'm going to be able to... I don't know, *catch him* or something, but he hits the ground before I can even close the distance between us.

"Fuuuuuuuck," he groans, sprawled on his back on the floor.

Rushing over, I throw my notebook and pen down onto the floor and drop to my knees by his head. "Oh my God. Are you okay? Are your legs broken? Can you wiggle your toes? Shit, I was just joking when I said I wanted to run you over with my car. I didn't actually want anything to happen to yo—"

"Emmie?" he says, low and rough, his eyes squeezed shut in pain.

I'm seriously worried he's broken something or he's going to have a concussion or something. As angry as he does make me, I definitely do not want anything to happen to him.

"Yes?" I say, leaning over him, running my hands over his torso to check for any bones or blood. We're so close I can feel his breath against my lips.

"I'm good, and as much as I'm glad that you didn't *actually* want me to die, can you let me up?"

Oh.

Ohhh.

"Yes. Of course, sorry!" I say, scrambling to my feet and extending my hand to him, which he bypasses and lifts himself off his back in one swift motion. For someone who just fell off a ladder and landed flat on his back, he sure recovered quickly.

He must read my expression because he chuckles, rolling his neck on his shoulders. "Not the first time I've fallen off a ladder. Won't be the last. Flattered that you're worried about me though."

"I... I was *not* worried. I was simply... protecting my asset. Because you know if you're dead, then this party can't happen, and I do not ever want to spend another night in that jail cell ever again."

"Sure," he hums, bending down to pick up his measuring tape, which fell in his scuffle. "Whatever you need to tell yourself to sleep better at night, Snowflake."

Snowflake. The new stupid nickname that definitely does not cause any kind of weird flurries in my stomach.

Absolutely not.

I've still got adrenaline pumping through my veins from nearly seeing death right in front of my eyes.

"Okay, well, moving right along. We've gotten most of the major points nailed down, but we'll need to discuss the smaller details more in depth. Unfortunately, I think we're going to have to make a trip to the city to get some of the things we need on such a short timeline."

That stops him in his tracks. "And when do you suppose that will happen? I have a big job that I'm trying to close."

I pull my calendar out of my bag and check the dates quickly. "I'm free this weekend? My clients had a last-minute trip scheduled, so it left me open."

Thankfully, most of my upcoming design jobs don't start until the New Year, so my schedule has more wiggle room than it normally would. Interior designer perks. Especially since I no longer offer holiday decorating for my clients so that I can do my own. Plus, now I have this party to handle.

Jackson pulls his phone out of his front pocket and swipes across the screen before dragging his gaze back to mine. "I can leave Friday afternoon, maybe around two."

Nodding, I jot the date down in my calendar with the right color-coded pen, ignoring the taunting smirk on his lips as I do. For someone who runs his own business, he seems sincerely opposed to any type of organization. "Sounds good to me. I can pick you up at your house at two?"

A low chuckle rumbles from his chest. "You can meet me at my house, but we're taking my truck."

"What? Absolutely *not*. My car is brand-new, and the heating is top-notch."

"And?" he asks, pocketing his phone. "Weather says there's a chance of heavy snow this weekend. It's nothing we haven't been through before, but my truck's equipped with tires for it, so it'll be safer if we take mine."

Sighing, I pinch the bridge of my nose. "I'm pretty sure you'd argue with me no matter what it was we were figuring out. My car has top-of-the-line safety features and is more than equipped to handle the snow. If it's some kind of masculinity thing that you're trying to prove, you know it won't kill you to let a woman drive you around."

This time, he laughs, shaking his head. "You're so fucking stubborn, you know that?"

"And you're not? I'm pretty sure you're the most stubborn man I've ever met."

"Look, I've got to get back to work. I'll see you Friday. My house. Two o'clock." He starts toward the door, and I call out, stopping him.

"At least take care of the hotel, okay? It'll be one less thing for me to worry about. And *two* rooms, please."

"Will do, Snowflake."

This is undoubtedly going to be the longest three weeks of my life.

8 /
jackson

Snowed in with Satan. **Santa

F riday rolled around quicker than I anticipated with how busy I've been trying to finish this project up before the holidays. I spent most of the week at my new build, avoiding my family like the plague.

Don't get me wrong, my brothers are my best friends, and my parents and I are unusually close-knit. And Josie... Well, she's just Josie. My ball of chaos baby sister.

We usually talk a few times a week, and there's a steady group text between all of us that never seems to let up.

But there's a reason that I've been avoiding them at all costs.

Emma Worthington.

After the day at the general store... and the night spent in jail, gossip spread through the entire town like wildfire. Which meant my phone was already blown up with texts and calls from my family before I even turned it back on once I was out.

I broke the news to my parents that we'd be having our annual party together with Emma's family, and they were not happy about it, but they realized there's no other choice, so they said whatever has to happen, we'll handle it. That's kind of just who my parents are.

They'll take anything and make the best of it. Just the way they did when this damn feud started in the first place. They took bad eggs and made eggnog. What's that saying again... when life gives you whatever?

So that's not why I'm avoiding them now. It's the fact that my mother likes to hover, and as much as I love her, I can't deal with all of her invasive questions while I'm also dealing with planning this stupid party. Not to mention, my brothers are having a fucking field day with the fact that I'm stuck working with Emma Worthington. And while I don't disagree with all of their shit-talking about the Worthingtons, I just don't have the time to listen to it. Because it won't help this party planning get done any faster.

The doorbell rings as I'm throwing clothes into my overnight bag, signaling Emma's arrival. Pausing, I walk to the front door and swing it open, revealing Emma on my doorstep.

She's got on a mouthwateringly tight pair of dark jeans paired with a formfitting cream sweater that I'm betting is cashmere and a matching beanie with a fluffy pom-pom on top.

She looks fucking *cute.*

And cute has never really been my thing, but then again, neither is sleeping with the enemy, yet here we are.

"Hi," she says, hoisting her designer bag, which seems packed to the seams, higher on her shoulder. I'm honestly surprised she hasn't toppled over from the weight of it.

Grinning, I reach out and take the bag, shockingly without any protest from her. "Hey. Come on in."

She steps over the threshold, and both Marley and Mo barrel toward her, each of them competing for her attention and all the head scratches they can get.

"Marley, Mo, chill out for a second and let her get through the door," I say sternly, shutting the front door and setting her bag on the floor. "You two rug rats act like you haven't been taught any manners."

"No, no, it's okay," she says, petting each of their heads gently, a giggle escaping when Marley licks her nose. "Gosh, you're both so cute. I can't even handle it."

Menaces. *Both* of them.

I drag my hand through my hair while they soak in all of her attention. "Let me grab my bag, and we can leave. Hopefully, we can make it into the city before dark."

She nods, not lifting her gaze from the dogs.

Jogging back to my room, I grab my bag and finish throwing everything I'll need in it for the next two days.

When I walk back into the living room, she's sitting on my couch, both dogs in her lap like they're tiny puppies and not the actual moose that they are.

Chuckling, I shake my head. "They've got you wrapped around their little paws. You know that, right?"

"Yeah, but it's nice. I wasn't allowed to have any animals growing up, and now that I, uh… I live alone, I haven't really ever considered getting a pet. Maybe I should."

"Yeah." I nod. "Maybe you should. Ready to go?"

She nods, giving them both one last pet and a kiss on their heads, then untangles herself from the couch and moves toward the front door to grab her bag.

I stop her just as she's about to grab it. "I got it."

Turning toward me, she looks surprised. "I thought you *weren't* a gentleman, Jackson Pearce?"

"Maybe I'm turning over a new leaf."

She hums as she opens the front door and steps outside. I follow behind her with both of our bags slung over my shoulder but pause as she walks toward her car.

"Fuck no, Emma. I told you we're taking my truck."

Her hands fly to her hips as she lifts a brow, a clear challenge. "I'm not arguing with you about this. We're taking *my* car, end of story."

Bypassing her completely, I walk over to my truck, wrench the door open, and put the bags on the floor of the cab, then turn it on and crank up the heat.

"Jackson, seriously. Do you *like* pissing me off?" she cries just as the first snow flurry begins to fall.

I hadn't noticed how much the temperature had dropped until now, the cold seeping through my jacket and causing my skin to prickle.

"Emma, get in the truck, or I will throw you over my fucking shoulder."

I know that's probably only going to make her more defiant, but fuck, it's freezing, and there is no goddamn way that I am getting in that tin can when a snowstorm is on the way. News says it shouldn't be that bad, but I'm not taking any chances.

Her jaw works, and her arms are crossed over her chest as she contemplates what I've said.

She should realize by now that I say what the fuck I mean.

When a few seconds pass and she makes no move, I take a

few steps toward her until I'm standing in front of her, and then I bend down and hoist her over my shoulder.

"Oh my God! You caveman, put me down!"

"Nope."

"Put me down, or I'm going to scream."

My shoulders shake with laughter. "Snowflake, there's not a neighbor for fucking miles. Scream all you want—no one's gonna hear you. Actually, better yet, let me give you an *actual* reason to scream. We both know how much you like to scream my name."

Her tiny fists hit my back, but I can barely even feel them through the thickness of my jacket.

"Enough," I say, slapping her directly on her jean-clad ass cheek, the sound echoing through the clearing. "It's cold as fuck, and I'm pretty sure my dick has shriveled inside me. We're taking my truck, end of fucking story."

Maybe it's the wind that suddenly seems to kick up just as I'm yanking the passenger door open and depositing her on the front seat, or maybe it's because she's decided to listen and stop being so damn stubborn for a single godforsaken second. But if I had to guess, it's the former, not the latter.

I wouldn't be lucky.

She squeaks as I toss her onto the seat and grab the seat belt, reaching over to buckle her in despite her protests. I shut the door and round the front to the driver's door before opening and sliding inside.

"Fuck, how did it get so cold so damn fast," I mutter, mostly to myself. My passenger princess grumbles under her breath but is otherwise silent.

Music to my ears.

Without another word, I put the truck in drive and head

down the driveway that leads off my property. At first glance, this place isn't much. Nothin' to write home about, for sure. But... what made me buy it in the first place is what you *don't* see.

You don't see bones, and those are the things that really matter.

Kind of that way with people too. It's what's *inside* that tells you everything you need to know about who a person truly is.

That house has a story behind it, and growing up, there was always a story being told. That it was haunted, that someone had been killed there, that there was a family of squatters living inside.

Nothing remotely close to the truth. It was abandoned after Dr. Jacobson lost his wife and then died of a broken heart.

It's a sad story, but when they showed me the house, Dr. Jacobson's son, Brent, told me to try and see all of the happiness that this house used to carry. To try and remember all of the laughter and the love that lived here before it became what it was later.

I'm not a sentimental kind of guy, but I was halfway sold when I heard that story, and the house itself did the rest.

I'm proud of all the work I've put in on it over the last couple of years.

"Can you please change it? I hate this song," Snowflake mumbles from the passenger seat. Her voice is so low that I can hardly hear it over the sound of the radio and the heater.

Snorting, I reach for the dial.

"What?"

"Nothing."

She huffs before she speaks. "Obviously something since you're... *snorting* like something's funny."

"You just seem like the kind of girl who wouldn't like George Straight."

"Just not my vibe. I was actually hoping to maybe turn it off so I could go over the list for the party? I just feel like I'm forgetting something." She rubs her fingers along her temples and sighs heavily.

Maybe I've been too busy trying to get a rise out of her to see how stressed she is, but I can feel it right now.

And apparently, I now give a shit about how Emma feels because I suddenly feel a little guilty for adding more to her plate.

"Hey, we'll get it figured out, alright? Don't stress over it," I say. "You don't have to do this by yourself. This is both of our punishment, not just yours."

I think that's the first time either of us has admitted that we were both at fault, not solely placing blame on the other.

She glances toward me, her lip between her teeth, and nods. "Thank you. I'm just... I'm feeling a lot of pressure to make sure everything goes according to plan. My parents are already disappointed, and I just don't want to let them down again. My dad is also still recovering from last year's... antics."

Damn, I didn't realize this party was that important to her. I mean, yeah, the feud has always been a thing, but judging simply by the expression on her face, I can tell that this is more to her than just a party. More than just not having charges pressed or a criminal record.

"I understand. Trust me, I get it. Don't worry, Snowflake."

"Thank you." Glancing down at her phone in her lap, she

chews at her painted nail as her eyes scan the screen. "Shit. Can you call the hotel and let them know we might miss check-in by a little? I think this storm actually might be getting worse based on the radar. Roads could be more hazardous than anticipated."

"Uh… what hotel?"

Emma's head whips up, her blue eyes shooting to mine. "Uh, the hotel that you were supposed to book? The one I told you to book when we were at Town Hall."

For a second, I rack my brain from the other day when we were together, and I'm coming up short. Fuck, I was exhausted that day, and quite frankly, the only thing I remember is Emma hovering over me, her plump pink lips just above mine after the ladder incident.

"Please," she starts, exhaling a deep breath. "*Please* tell me you did not forget to book the hotel, Jackson."

"I didn't."

"Oh, thank God. I was about t—" she says, but my words cut her off.

"Okay, I *didn't book it*, but in my defense, I didn't hear you even ask me to in the first place, so I *technically* didn't forget."

She groans next to me, and I feel her head hit the headrest of the old bench seat behind her. "This is a disaster. An absolute, complete freakin' disaster."

Keeping my eyes on the road, I tell her, "It's okay. Surely, we'll find something once we get into town. We'll just wing it."

I turn my wipers up. The snow is falling more heavily, and it's dark now, making it nearly impossible to see the road in front of me. The further we get from town, the worse the roads will be since they won't have been cleared or salted.

We've been on the road now for thirty minutes, and I knew that if it came down to it, my truck would be safer. Sturdier.

Harder to dent.

But what I wasn't accounting for was how quickly the weather would decline.

"God, wing it? In the middle of a snowstorm? That's if we even make it there!" she cries. "Look how hard it's snowing, Jackson. The roads aren't going to be safe much longer. The only place between here and town is the old motel off of Highway 55, so if we miss it, then there's nothing for another thirty miles. This is *exactly* why I had a plan, why you can't just 'wing it.' Why can't you take my plans more seriously?"

Shit, she's right—there's nothing for miles after we pass there. Lord fucking knows I don't want to get caught out here in this cold. And even if we somehow made it to the city, it would take forever, and the roads would be just as bad there. And who knows if we could even find a place to stay?

"Looks like we're stopping at the motel for the night, then, Snowflake."

A heavy sigh leaves her lips as she glances back down at her phone in her lap. "My battery is almost dead, and *of course* this truck is so old it doesn't even have a place to charge it. God, if you would've been less caveman-y and more logical, we could've taken my car and not had to worry about whether or not we're going to freeze to death overnight in the middle of a freaking *blizzard*, Jackson!"

From a snowstorm to a blizzard. Got it.

I let her get all her frustration out because it was clearly simmering below the surface, especially after the stuff she just shared about her parents, and when she's done, she squeezes her eyes shut, taking another deep breath.

"It'll be fine. Look, there's the motel up there." I gesture through the snow-covered windshield to the bright red blinking sign that actually only says "tel" since the other two letters have gone out.

I can practically feel the exasperation coming off her in waves, but I'm not going to take a chance with our lives on these roads, driving my truck or not. It's gotten bad, quickly.

Pulling my truck into the parking lot, I put it in park before turning to her. "I'm going to go see if they have any rooms available."

"They better have a room available, Jackson Pearce. For your sake." Her lips are twisted into a frown.

Not sure whether or not I should be afraid of Emma right now or turned on, but it's definitely a mixture of both.

I pull my old ball cap further down my ears like it will somehow stop the cold from seeping past the mesh, and then I step out into the snow. The ground is so fucking slick I almost eat shit right by the front door of the office but somehow manage to wrench the door open and step inside. Thank fuck, I'm immediately hit with a gust of warmth.

"Hiya, darlin'!" an older lady with graying hair says from the other side of the desk. She's working on what looks to be like knitting a sweater.

"Hi, do you have any rooms available? That storm really came out of nowhere."

She nods, looking up from her yarn and offering me a kind smile. "Yes, it did seem to come out of nowhere. Don't worry, sweetheart, we'll get you situated. What type of room are you looking for?"

"Two, if possible."

"Ah." Her eyes flit down the ledger in front of her, her brow furrowing closely after. "It seems like we only have one room available left tonight. We had quite a few people stopping in when they heard of the storm, and of course, we had to reserve a few rooms for our staff. Don't want them traveling on the roads in this weather either."

I nod. "Of course not. I'll take it."

Reaching into my pocket, I pull out cash from my wallet since something tells me that they don't have a card machine, judging by the paper ledger she's using.

Gwen, I learn her name is, quickly checks us in, then hands me an old motel key and directs me where to park. We say a quick goodbye, and I open the door and face the cold once more.

Emma is glowering at me from the front seat, her arms crossed over her chest.

Too bad she doesn't know that there's only one room available tonight, with one single bed.

It's going to be a long night.

And not in the way I'd hoped.

9 /
emma

Hallmark after dark

"You've *got* to be kidding me," I say, my eyes widening as I follow behind Jackson into the room.

Singular room.

Because of course that would be how it happens, especially when involving Jackson Pearce.

Only one *single room* left at this motel.

Even better?

It's the honeymoon suite, complete with decor straight from the eighties, with a matching red heart-shaped Jacuzzi tub directly in its center.

"Nice," he says, completely unfazed.

I feel like I'm the star of some reality television show and not a part of the joke that everyone else seems to be in on but me.

"Jackson, we can't possibly stay here," I tell him exasperatedly. "Surely, you realize that, right?"

His brows rise. "Where else are we going to stay, Snowflake?"

I take a second to take some calming deep breaths and try

to recenter myself. My eyes flit around the room as I take in the velvet quilt and pale pink sheets on the bed to the Jacuzzi tub that has two heart-shaped towels linked together next to it, along with a cheap bottle of champagne.

"You're right. Sorry, I'm just stressed, but also, this *is* your fault for not booking the room," I say, walking over and sitting on the edge of the bed, pulling my phone out of my purse. I need to at least text my parents and my best friend, Katie, to let them know that I'm safe. Well, as safe as I can be, considering I now have to share a bed overnight with someone who probably wants to suffocate me in my sleep or fuck me. It changes by the minute.

No, no, no. We are not going there tonight. I'm not even going to think about the last time that Jackson and I spent the night together. I'm definitely not going to think about how he looked with me on my knees between his strong, muscled thighs with his hands tangled in my hair and the strong column of his throat exposed as he groaned in pleasure.

I'm definitely not going to think about that. Just like there's definitely not an ache forming between my thighs right at this very moment.

"You good? Your cheeks are flushed."

I nod, avoiding his gaze as I stand from the bed to grab my overnight bag and start to dig inside of it for my clothes. "Yup. Totally fine. Just going to get ready for bed. I'm tired."

"Okay, no problem. I'm going to go look for a vending machine for dinner since I'm sure everything is closed. Any requests?"

Looking up, my gaze travels over the expanse of his shoulders, drinking in the way the fabric of his shirt hugs the muscles, and it makes me wonder if he works out.

Does he spend time in the gym, or are those muscles simply the result of all the manual labor he does with his job?

"Anything is fine for me. A water would be great."

He nods and, with one last look, disappears through the motel door, leaving me in silence, and for the first time tonight, I feel like I can take a full breath.

I quickly slip into the bathroom and put on the only thing I brought to sleep in, which is a big T-shirt and a pair of panties because, of course, I didn't think I'd be sharing a room with anyone. Especially not *him*.

It's either this... or sleeping in my jeans, which is not happening. Jackson is just going to have to get over it and learn how to be the gentleman he always seems to make fun of.

Do I actually even like when he's a gentleman though? Truly? Because I seem to love this rough, unruly version of him, even though I shouldn't.

Groaning, I drop my head in my hands before lifting it to stare into the small mirror above the sink. My blonde hair is half-damp, half-dry from the snow, a tangled mess framing my face. I bypassed a full face of makeup today except for a smidge of BB cream, mascara, and lip gloss, so I grab a rag and wipe off the remnants.

Once I'm done, I brush my teeth and run my hairbrush through my hair, then remove my contacts and put on my glasses.

I usually only wear them before bed, so it'll be the first time that Jackson's seen me in them.

Not that I'm worried about what he thinks of my appearance or anything.

Because I'm most definitely *not*. Besides, it's pretty clear that he's attracted to me, which is a whole problem in and of itself.

Smoothing my hands down over my nightshirt, I open the door and find Jackson sitting in the chair, a bag of chips opened in front of him as he's bent over what looks like house plans.

"Bathroom's open if you need it," I say, making my way to the bed and pulling back the covers.

"Thanks. I was just going over these plans again. We're close to finishing, and I want to make sure everything's perfect," he says as he rolls up the paper and puts it back into his bag.

"For a new house?"

He nods. "Yeah, one of the biggest custom builds I've ever done. A lot of moving parts to make a house come together." Grabbing the pile of snacks from the table, he walks over and flops down across from me, spreading the pile out. "I didn't know what to get, so I got a bit of everything. I'm a chocolate kinda guy."

"You seem like a chocolate kind of guy."

For a second, he looks offended. "What's that supposed to mean, Snowflake?"

I shrug. "I dunno, you just seem like the kind of guy that likes chocolate over... sour stuff? I think you can tell a lot about a person by the kind of candy they like."

His chuckle shakes the bed beneath us as I lean up and pull my T-shirt over my legs, sitting crisscross.

"You're not the kinda girl I could imagine sharing vending machine food with in a tacky honeymoon suite, but there's a first time for everything, huh?"

I glance around again, my nose scrunching slightly at the

red carpet and matching curtains before I look back at Jackson, who's watching me with an amused smile on his face. "I mean, it's not really that bad. It could definitely be worse. Maybe it's even growing on me a little bit."

Not at all, but he doesn't have to know that.

With a cheeky smirk, I swipe the chocolate bar out of his hand as he's bringing it to his mouth and take a bite.

"All of this candy here, and you want what I've got, Emmie?" he teases.

"Sorry, but yours is better. I meant to ask you... how did your parents take the news? Finding out about the party?"

He shrugs. "They weren't overjoyed with the fact, but honestly? What else can we do? We're all stuck in the situation and having to try and make the best of it."

I nod. "I wish my parents felt that way. I mean, I feel like the disappointment of a century, but what's new, right?"

Jackson's brow furrows, and he takes the candy bar back from me, taking a bite, then mumbles around the mouthful, "Why would you be a disappointment to them?"

"I don't know. I just... I constantly feel like I'm always falling short. My parents just have really high expectations for how I should act, and what I should wear, and how I should behave, and sometimes it just feels so heavy. Moments like the other day with my mom. Sorry, you probably don't care about any of that." I huff a laugh and drag my gaze off his.

It feels weird, yet oddly cathartic, to admit that out loud to Jackson.

Then, I feel his fingers on my chin, turning my eyes back to his. "I do care, Emma. You're not a disappointment to anyone, and if your parents think that, then they're blind. You're beautiful, smart, and ambitious."

I can feel my cheeks heat under his praise, and I swallow down the emotion that's bundled tightly in my throat. "Thank you. That was sweet of you to say."

"Just the truth." His voice drops an octave as his eyes roam the expanse of my legs that have come out of the T-shirt.

God, how is it possible that I somehow feel the heat of his gaze on me? Like he's reached out and ghosted his fingers along the places his eyes have roamed.

It's impossible, yet I can feel my skin heating without a single touch.

"Jackson…" I warn.

"Emmie."

"Don't look at me like that."

His brow arches, feigning innocence as he sets down the candy. "And how am I looking at you?"

He knows exactly the way he's looking at me.

In a way he shouldn't be looking at me because we said one night, and we said we'd never speak of it again.

Even if… it seems like neither of us *truly* wants that.

"Like you want to touch me."

Leaning closer, he whispers, "How do I want to touch you, Snowflake?"

God, just the deep, gravelly baritone of his voice makes my clit throb. The power he has over me should be concerning, but the man makes me crazy, out of my mind horny for him.

"We can't do this, Jackson. Things are already so complicated… The party…" I swallow, my heart speeding up in my chest as his fingers dance along the hem of my faded T-shirt, brushing against my skin and making me shiver. "Our parents... our families' history. This is a distraction we can't afford. I mean, we don't even like each other."

He chuckles humorously. "Yeah, well, I think I like you more than I should. I *can't* stop fucking thinking about you. Don't you think it would be easier if I didn't see your perfect little pussy every time I close my eyes? If I could stop remembering for a single second how you came on my cock or the way you fit me so goddamn tight, like you were made for me?" With that, he scoots closer, and before I know it, I'm on my back, and he's fitted his hips between my thighs, hovering over me as he continues. "My life would be a hell of a lot easier if I hadn't started to realize that maybe I have a thing for this sassy, overly organized, takes no shit and gives it back twofold girl."

I blink, fisting my hands into the sheets so I don't do something stupid like touch him. "That sounds a lot like me."

Laughing, he leans down and drags his nose along my jaw, causing my breath to hitch. "Yeah. That's exactly who you are, Snowflake, and I think I fucking like it. I like it a lot."

This would be the time to stop. To sit up, get my thoughts straight, and tell him that we're done... doing *whatever* it is we're doing.

Except when his hand slides underneath the fabric of my shirt and his fingers ghost along the hem of my panties, I know that there is no way that is happening.

There's not a chance in Santa's freakin' winter wonderland that I am telling this man no. Not when he lights me on fire like this.

This... pull between us is just too strong. I've never wanted *anything* in my life as badly as I want Jackson Pearce.

Not the man I knew as my nemesis.

But the man I'm beginning to realize has more to him than I ever imagined.

As if reading my mind, he rasps, "Let's worry about the rest later. Right now, all I want to do is taste you, Emma." Lifting my shirt, he holds my eyes intently. "I want to feel you come on my cock again. I want to spend the rest of the night forgetting the world until it's just you and I."

I nod, helping him pull the baggy T-shirt over my head and discard it, leaving me in nothing but lace.

"You and these fucking panties. Pink and frilly, just like you." His words are a grunt as he tears them from my body with a swift pull, much like the last time.

I'm beginning to think this man has a fetish for ripping my panties.

He licks his lips, then bites down on his bottom lip as his eyes roam my body, sending a bolt of arousal through me. Why is that so hot?

The man is looking at me like I'm his next meal.

"I'm committing this to memory, Snowflake. Every single inch of you." His slow perusal stops in between my thighs, and his hands slide up, parting them so he gets a full view of my pussy.

I already know I'm wet and throbbing just by the way his gaze makes me ache.

Reaching behind his neck, he quickly pulls his shirt off and throws it to the side.

My mouth waters at the sight of his broad chest, chiseled abs, the delicious dips of his Adonis belt. The man looks like he stepped right out of a magazine, not from a construction site.

I drag my eyes down every sharp line of his muscles, stopping at the trail of hair leading below his waistband.

"Now, who's looking at who?" He grins, unbuckling his belt and flicking his jeans open with one hand. He pulls the belt free with one powerful tug.

Dear God.

"I wonder what you'd look like with my belt around your wrists? On your knees like the good girl you are, taking my cock. Mmm." His eyes search around the room, and his brow arches when it lands on the small Christmas tree in the corner.

Standing from the bed, he walks to the tree, plucks a thick red satin ribbon from the branches, and turns to me. "How about we play with *this* instead, Snowflake?"

My heart races when I imagine him... *tying* me up with that, and my entire pussy throbs in response to the mental picture. A visceral reaction that I couldn't control even if I wanted to.

God, I am such a slut for this man.

He could play with me however he wanted, and I'd probably agree.

When I nod, he walks back to the bed with the ribbon fisted in his hands, his pants hanging open, the bulge of his cock tenting beneath his briefs.

"On your knees," he commands, low and rough.

I roll onto my stomach without hesitation and lift up on my hands and knees, hiking my ass high in the air. I can feel his eyes on my ass, on the pulsing spot between my legs, as he comes to a halt behind me. The heat of his body makes me squirm in anticipation of what's to come.

His hand meets the curve of my hip, sliding to the front of

my stomach and up to my breasts, where he pinches my sensitive nipple between his fingers. Taking his time, he rolls the peak between his fingers roughly, then slides his hand higher to my throat, where he grasps lightly, lifting me off my hands till I'm sitting up on my knees.

"Wrists, Snowflake."

Three syllables is all it takes for wetness to coat my thighs.

Obediently, I put my wrists behind my back, and I feel his fingers brush along the skin inside. He leans forward, gently pressing his fingers to my throat as his lips ghost against the shell of my ear. "If at any time you want me to take the ribbon off, say stop and I'll remove it. Okay?"

I nod.

"I need to hear you say it, Emma. Do you understand?"

"Yes," I breathe. "I understand."

Gathering my wrists in his hands, I feel the soft satin of the ribbon brush against my skin as he fastens it on my wrists, binding them together.

"Good girl. This is for your pleasure," he murmurs as he lowers me to the bed with my cheek pressed into the mattress. "Feel okay?"

"Yes. Feels perfect."

He gently spreads my legs apart, and then I feel the hot wash of his breath against my core. I'm so turned on, so needy, so desperate for his touch that I'm not above begging.

Palming my ass, he spreads me open. "Tell me what you need."

"Your... Your mouth. Please."

His chuckle vibrates against my skin, and I whimper at the sensation.

"Only because you asked *so* nicely."

His tongue drags through my wetness from my clit to my ass, lapping at me over and over until I'm writhing, my nails cutting into my palms as I push back against his mouth.

It's obscene and dirty, the way he's eating me from behind, my face pressed into the mattress and my hands bound.

I want *more*.

My back arches when he latches onto my clit and sucks, his teeth scraping against me lightly. It's a foreign sensation, but it feels so good that I'm already dancing on the edge of an orgasm, and I cry out, unable to keep quiet.

I'm rocking back on my knees, desperate for the pleasure building inside of me. Higher. Higher. Higher.

"I'm going to…" I pant breathlessly. His finger circles my entrance and pushes inside, the blunt pad immediately finding my G-spot and stroking until my vision dances.

Black spots flicker behind my eyes, and my eyelids drop shut.

"God… Jackson…*Please*."

He's fucking me with his finger at the same rhythm that his tongue flicks my clit, swirling his tongue when he sucks it into his mouth.

I come harder than I ever have in my life, on the edge of a blackout, my entire body shaking as he uses his skilled mouth and finger to coax it out of me. He never stops caressing the spot inside of me that prolongs my orgasm until I'm limp and my body feels completely boneless.

It's… *never b*een this way for me, and somehow, Jackson does it effortlessly.

"I want another from you," he says. "Can you do that for me, Snowflake?"

Another? Right now, I'm not even sure I can move, but I nod.

I hear the rustle of fabric, and then the bed dips behind me as he gently pulls me up until my back is flush with his front and his fingers are gently pressed against my throat.

A kink I never realized I had until now.

"I want to see you take my cock the way you take my fingers. Stretching around me while I fill you with my cum."

Using his free hand, he drags the thick head of his cock through my pussy lips, coating his length with wetness, once, then again before he rocks his hips, rutting against my clit. The sensation causes my back to arch, and at that moment, he thrusts to the hilt inside me, both of us groaning in unison.

"Fuck, you're perfect," he groans, dropping his lips to my neck and sucking at the sensitive skin below my ear. I shiver as he withdraws his cock and surges forward again, thrusting hard. With each slap of his hips, my breasts sway, and I ache to reach up and touch my nipples.

He reaches to my front, circling my clit roughly, the sound of our hips meeting reverberating around us, creating an obscene symphony that sends me barreling toward an orgasm I wasn't sure I could have. Not after the one he's already coaxed from me.

This man has learned exactly what my body needs, and he's using it as the most delicious tool.

With the combination of his hips rocking in rough, deep strokes and the feel of his fingers strumming my clit, I freefall into pleasure.

I feel him drop his forehead against my shoulder, his teeth finding my skin as he bites down and groans, coming inside of me.

The bite of pain, mixed with pleasure, pulls my body taut as we come together, his hand at my throat and the other still circling my hypersensitive clit until I'm sagging against him, unable to hold myself up any longer.

That's when I realize, with the thrashing of my heart in my chest, the flutter of my pulse, the ribbon binding my wrists, the feel of his lips along my skin... that there won't be any going back to how it was before Jackson.

10 /
jackson

Green is not my color

Light peeks through the heavy velvet curtains, and even though I know it's time to get up so we can get back on the road, I want to stay in the warmth of this bed with Emmie's naked body wrapped around me. I want to pretend like this stupid damn party doesn't exist and that once we leave, real life isn't going to come crashing back in.

Because the moment we step outside of these doors, we'll go back to pretending we hate each other, not like together we have the best sex of our lives. Not like it seems we don't really hate each other at all.

Maybe it's because the longer I spend with Emma, the more I realize that I had it all wrong. She's the opposite of everything I expected her to be. Maybe it's because I'm the only one that Emma feels like she can be less than perfect with. Her true self, unashamedly, without having to put up the wall she's built around her heart in the process.

"Good morning," Emma's soft, sleepy voice murmurs from the crook of my neck, where she's nestled.

"Morning, Snowflake."

My voice is still heavy with sleep, and I make no move to get up, instead tightening my arms around her.

"As much as I don't want to, we've gotta get a move on it if we're planning on accomplishing anything other than orgasms this weekend."

I feel her lips turn up against my skin, and I press mine to her hair in a chaste kiss, then tuck the covers around her and head to the bathroom.

Something tells me that after last night, she's going to need a moment to... process. Clearly, there was a shift, and I don't know how she's going to feel about it. I just know I can't be the only one who felt that. So while I'm showering, I'll give her a minute to work through her head, and then we'll spend the rest of the day checking things off her list.

Emma

"I HONESTLY FORGET how much I love the city until I come to visit," I say, tucking my hands into the pockets of my jacket. "It's beautiful. The buildings, all of the decorations for Christmas."

Jackson nods. "Would you ever move here? Leave Strawberry Hollow?"

"Oh gosh, no. I mean, it's beautiful, don't get me wrong, but I am a firm believer that home is where the heart is. My parents are there, my friends, my job. I wouldn't know how to be anywhere else."

"Yeah, same. I thought about it. Leaving," he says as we walk down the crowded sidewalk. Snow is falling lightly around us, and the smell of candied pecans hangs in the air from the booths lining the busy city street, a small reminder of home. "Back before I decided to start Pearce Builders. I thought about getting out while I could, and then I realized that nowhere would ever be home the way Strawberry Hollow is."

I nod. "It has a funny way of working its way into your heart and making it impossible for you to leave."

"Yeah." He smiles. "So, what are we checking off today?"

I take my phone out of my bag and pull up the list I've been compiling since our meeting at Town Hall, trying not to feel overwhelmed and completely out of control about the party that is creeping up on us. "Um, we need to find a band, go to the florist, meet with the bakery, and then figure out all of the little details. Remaining decorations, table settings, etcetera etcetera. Get anything we need to have delivered for the party since this is the only time we'll be able to come into the city."

"Lead the way."

Hours later, we've checked approximately two things off our list: the band and simple floral arrangements for the tables.

Now for the hard part.

"We are not having a six-tier vanilla cake, Emmie. Jesus, that has to be the most boring shit ever invented." He leans closer, his lips brushing against the shell of my ear as he whispers, "And now I know there's nothing *vanilla* about you. Especially not after last night."

The low timbre of his voice causes my thighs to clench and my clit to throb when I think of that ribbon and all of the deliciously dirty things he did to my body without an ounce of shame.

Needless to say, even though I was not originally over-joyed about being stuck in a honeymoon suite with Jackson Pearce, we christened it in more ways than one.

"Jackson!" I exclaim, my eyes darting around to see if anyone heard him. "*Behave*. We have to get through this list, and we will never make it if you don't act like a... gentleman."

His lip tugs into a cocky grin, but he keeps his comments to himself, even though I know it's killing him.

"Fine, since you obviously have an... *aversion* to vanilla. What do you suggest?"

"Hmmm... what about gingerbread?"

Biting my lip, I mull it over. That's actually... not a bad idea.

"I'm listening."

The sexy smirk on his lips widens into a full-blown smile that has the ability to knock me clean off my feet, or at least the breath from my lungs.

He's so handsome and so, *so* far off-limits it's not even part of the picture.

Mind-blowing orgasms? That's one thing, but these feel-ings... they're a completely new ball game.

The last thing we need to complicate this even further is feelings. We're just two consenting adults having very hot, very delicious sex in private, and when everyone's around, we're two people who have always hated each other.

Nothing more, nothing less.

"Where'd you go?" he asks.

Blinking, I shake my head, refocusing on him as we stand in the bakery. "Sorry, zoned out. What did you say?"

He squints. "I said, what if we did a gingerbread-flavored cake with white icing so it matches your 'aesthetic.'" He lifts his fingers in quotes. "This bakery has the best gingerbread cake from here to the coast. Trust me."

I nod.

He walks to the front counter and greets the woman working behind it, a bright smile on his face as he talks to her. She's enamored by him from the very first word, and God, do I understand. It's impossible not to fall for his charm.

After a few moments, they both walk over to where I'm standing.

"Hi! I'm Avery, and I was just talking to Jackson, and he filled me in on your Christmas party, which is so cute, by the way! He said you're the brains behind the operation, so I just wanted to run a few ideas I have by you?"

"Yes, of course," I tell her, plastering on a smile, even though I'm feeling slightly irrationally jealous at the way she keeps glancing at Jackson and batting her eyelashes.

"Okay, cool. We can sit here if you'd like. Give me just a sec to grab my pen and a book." She sashays away, her perky little ponytail bouncing as she goes, and I sit back, crossing my arms over my chest, completely avoiding Jackson's gaze.

Avery returns a minute later with a giant binder, notebook, and pencils, then pulls out the chair, sits down, and immediately dives into her ideas for the party cake. Even if she had to pause a few times to smile at Jackson and made sure to put her hand on his stupid veiny forearms more than once, her ideas are good, and I think they did a good job of translating what we both wanted into something feasible.

"It was so nice to meet you guys," she says, closing the binder and rising from her chair. "Here's my card, and my number is on the back if you need it. For anything."

She says it provocatively, as she's staring directly at Jackson with clear interest, and I honestly don't know what's come over me today. I step closer to him, my fingers lacing into his as I smile at her. "Of course. I'll reach out if I have any questions. Thank you so much, Avery."

For a second, she can't hide the soured expression on her face, but as quickly as it came, it's gone, and her cheery smile is replaced. "You bet! Thanks!"

I notice in our exchange that Jackson doesn't pull away. If anything, he tightens his fingers in mine and stands next to me with an amused expression on his face.

In fact, he doesn't say anything at all as I drop his hand and walk out of the bakery onto the sidewalk out front. Only *then* does he speak.

"What was that, Emmie?"

Avoiding his gaze, I pick at the pink paint on my nails, which is looking far more appealing than admitting to him what that was back there. "Not sure what you mean, Jackson."

He steps forward and grabs my hand, stilling my fingers before he tips my chin up so my eyes are on his. "Were you jealous?"

"Yeah, right," I scoff, but my throat feels thick as I try to swallow down the foreign feeling. "As if."

I focus on the smokey ring of his irises and not how much I love the way he smells, how his hard body is pressed against mine in the middle of a busy street, or how my body reacts to his with only his proximity.

"I think you were jealous, Snowflake. And you know what that tells me?"

"Mmm?"

He leans in an inch closer until his lips almost brush mine. "That you want me, and not *just* for my cock."

As much as I try to stifle it, the shiver that runs down my spine is an involuntary reaction to the word *cock* in that deep, husky baritone of his.

I open my mouth to protest his silly accusation, but his thumb darts out, and the pad of it drags along my bottom lip. The protest dies on my tongue, and I swallow hard.

"I think that you're not used to the feeling. And it terrifies you as much as thrills you."

My gaze still fixed on his, I whisper, "I think you're *delusional*, Jackson Pearce."

Except he's not, and I hate admitting that he's right.

11 /
jackson
My favorite present

"Fine, you pick out an ugly Christmas sweater with me, and I'll *watch* you ice-skate," I say, my arms crossed over my chest.

Her eyes roll. "I'll come with you to pick out a sweater if you *come* ice-skating with me."

Damn woman.

One thing we agreed to disagree about for this party is the fact that she wanted cocktail attire, and I wanted something my family has been doing for decades. Ugly sweaters.

It's a Pearce tradition. *The uglier, the better.*

And not only is it a tradition, but it's *fun*, which I think Emma needs more of.

At one point last night, I got her to agree by eating her pussy until she was too spent to do any arguing. And now her answer stands.

The invitation that is going out on Monday will say cocktail *or* ugly sweater attire, and even though it seems like a frivolous thing, this includes something both of our families would want.

105

"Deal," I say as we head in the direction of a department store. I pause and grab her hand, sliding it in mine. It feels... natural. Holding her hand and walking down the street together without everyone's eyes on us. Here, we're just two people holding hands, but at home... I think we might actually stop traffic if someone saw us walking down Main Street hand in hand.

It might not be anyone's business, but that wouldn't stop the gossip.

"You know, I've been thinking." I glance over at her, my eyes raking over her cheeks, which are pink from the cold. She looks fucking adorable with her beanie on and flurries of snow clinging to her lashes. "I think we should spend the rest of the day enjoying the city. Having fun. Before we head back to Strawberry Hollow tomorrow."

"There's no way. We have so much to do for the part—" she starts, but I stop walking and turn to face her, cradling her jaw in my hand.

My thumb sweeps along her cheek. "You deserve a day of fun, Emma. Look, you've been working around the clock to make this party happen. You've gotten the decorations. We've booked the cake, found the bartender, booked a band. We've checked a lot off your list. A single evening off is not going to unravel all of the progress made. The rest of the day, you're mine, okay?"

For a second, I think she may say no, that she's not interested in being mine for any length of time, even if it is only for a day.

Until recently, I never realized that Emma carried so much pressure on her shoulders. I spent all my life thinking she was an uptight, pretentious princess who was too good for anyone else, but now that I've gotten the chance to actually know her, I realize that I was wrong. Sure, she's a perfectionist. She wants everything to be organized and in order, but she's also hardworking and passionate when she cares about something. She's been open to compromise and finding a solution that would make *both* of our families happy. Not just hers. And when she lets loose, she's a lot of fun too.

There's more to Emma Worthington than meets the eye, and I want to know everything that she doesn't show the world.

"You know, I don't think we're very good at the whole *one time* thing, Jackson," she whispers, her eyes holding mine. "We're two and oh right now."

My shoulder dips. "Maybe we just need more practice, Snowflake. C'mon. Give me one day."

She tilts her head to the side and scrunches her nose up, clearly pretending to consider my request when we both know she'll agree.

"Okay. *One* day."

I can't help the smile that lifts my lips, and I sure as hell don't even try. I've got one day to make her smile, to remind her that there's more to Christmas than just this damn party, to do the things that make *her* happy. Things that *don't* include a to-do list. If she wants to go ice-skating, then fuck it, I guess I'm going ice-skating.

Before I can stop myself, I press a chaste kiss to her lips, then grasp her hand in mine. "One day. Let's do this."

"DEAR GOD, THAT IS ABSOLUTELY *HIDEOUS*," Emma says when I walk out of the dressing room, her nose scrunched in distaste. "Please tell me you are *not* thinking about buying that."

"Oh baby, it's coming home with me." I smirk, doing a full three-sixty so she can see the back, "And you're getting one too."

"I'm pretty sure my mother would burn it if I walked in wearing that." She giggles, her whole face lighting up.

Fuck, I love that sound more than I ever thought I could.

Choosing the ugliest sweater in this place to make her laugh: mission accomplished.

She's not wrong. It truly is fucking hideous, but then again, isn't that the point? The uglier, the better.

It's bright red and covered in sparkly gold tinsel adorned with large green bells that jingle every time I move.

"Go try yours on. I need proof that I actually got Emma Worthington into an ugly sweater," I say with a wink.

Emma rolls her eyes but stands from the chair across from the dressing room, taking off her suede peacoat and leaving it there. "God, I can't believe I'm even doing this, but here we go."

I take a seat in the chair, the bells on the sweater jingling as I do. Okay, it might be a little annoying, but it's festive as fuck, so I'm keeping it.

Once she's inside the dressing room, I pull out my phone and open my notifications. It's been going off nonstop since we left, but aside from a check-in text to let my family know that I was safe after the storm, I haven't responded.

It's actually been kind of nice to unplug for a bit, even if it's only for a weekend. Not something I normally am able to do with how busy my company stays.

"Crap. Jackson?" I hear from the other side of the dressing room door. "Uh, I think my hair is stuck on the tag. Can you, uh, come help me? My hair is stuck in this hideous thing."

I stand from the chair, pocketing my phone and crossing the room in a few short strides, the fucking bells on the sweater still jingling with each step as I slip inside the dressing room and shut the door as quietly as I can.

Which isn't very fucking quiet since I'm basically a walking, noise-making Christmas decoration.

Emma's standing in front of the mirror, her cheeks bright red, a contrast from the green sweater she's wearing that has a Christmas tree that's got blinking lights and ornaments and says *"GET LIT"* across the front.

"Damn, Snowflake. You look hot as *fuck.*" Reaching up carefully, I gingerly sweep her hair off her neck and untangle the lock of hair that's wrapped around the tag, freeing her. "Not going to lie, my dick's getting hard just seeing you look so… *festive*. Really does it for me," I tease. I'm joking, but fuck, not really. I am *definitely* into her like this.

She giggles. "I've honestly never felt more ridiculous in my life."

"Nah. You look good enough to eat, Snowflake." I lick my lips as my eyes rake down her body and then back up in slow appreciation.

Her gaze turns hazy at my words, and I step closer, slowly walking her backward until her back hits the mirror behind her. My fingers tease along the hem of her top, then dip beneath the fabric, brushing along her skin.

I love seeing her like this, relaxed and carefree. Having

fun without worrying about a schedule or a list. Which gives me an idea…

"How about a little Christmas fun day… *bet*?" I continue sliding my hand up her stomach, ghosting along her rib cage to the cup of her bra, where I finger the lace.

The column of her throat bobs as she swallows, watching me through wide eyes. "W-what kind of bet?"

Instead of answering, I flip her around to face the mirror, her gaze roaming over the two of us in the reflection. Me standing behind her with my hands beneath the sweater, her cheeks flushed and her eyes heavily lidded as her chest heaves as I brush my thumb over her nipple.

My fingers on my other hand flick open the button of her jeans and dip beneath the fabric, sweeping along the lace of her panties.

"'I'm going to make you come on my face, right here in this dressing room," I rasp against the shell of her ear, nipping at the lobe. "And if you make a sound, then you're wearing that sweater for the rest of the day."

Her eyes drop shut when I hook my fingers in the waist-band of her jeans and work them down along with the scrap of lace covering her pussy just enough to where her ass is exposed.

"Hands on the mirror, Emma. Eyes on me. I want you to watch me eat your perfect little pussy. And I need you to be a good girl and be quiet, or everyone on the other side of that door is going to know what I'm doing. That you're soaking my face."

She nods breathlessly, our eyes connecting in the mirror as she bends forward, resting her hands on the glass, arching her back, and giving me the perfect fucking view of her pert ass and wet pussy.

Fuck, my mouth waters, seeing her pink and glistening.

I drop to my knees behind her, using my thumbs to spread her open wide as my gaze rakes hungrily from the tight ring of her ass to her entrance and then to her clit.

She's fucking *exquisite*, an actual work of art, and I'm desperate for a taste.

When my tongue flicks her clit, her pussy contracts, and it's the hottest fucking thing I've ever seen.

I palm her ass, squeezing the globes within my fists as I lean forward and latch onto her clit, sucking it into my mouth with fervor, alternating with pressure from my tongue until her hips are writhing against my mouth. I bring my eyes to the mirror, staring at her reflection, making sure she's containing her moans and not getting us caught before I can get her off.

Emma is *beautiful*. Effortlessly so. She commands attention from the moment she steps into a room.

But like this?

Cheeks flushed, her lips parted, her eyes squeezed shut in ecstasy. Completely uninhibited and trusting that I'll take care of her?

She's so breathtaking that it makes my head feel dizzy with desire for her.

My finger circles her entrance, pushing in an inch, only for her to let out the softest whimper I've ever heard. Her eyes fly open, connecting with mine as she pulls her lip between her teeth, biting it.

"Your pussy is dripping, Snowflake. Such a good, *dirty* girl, taking my finger. Does it turn you on knowing anyone could hear us? Knowing anyone could walk in and see you bent over, your tight little pussy on display, swallowing up my fingers?"

She slams her hips back when I add another finger, stroking her G-spot until I can feel her legs trembling. I lap at her clit in sync with my fingers, whispering praise against her slick skin.

I can feel when she starts to tighten around my fingers, her pussy clamping down, trying to suck my fingers in.

Knock, knock, knock.

We both freeze at the interruption. Emma's eyes fly open, and her expression turns panicked.

"Hi! Is everything okay in there?" the saleswoman says from the other side of the door. "I'd be happy to grab you another size if you need?"

I smirk against Emma's skin, then flatten my tongue and drag it up through her wetness. She drops her forehead against the mirror loudly, a moan leaving her lips as I plunge my fingers back inside of her, deep and hard.

Her attempts at biting back her breathless moans are now fruitless, so I stand and reach for her, pulling her back from the mirror and sliding my fingers that were just buried deep inside her into her mouth, commanding, "Suck."

Never mind the woman on the other side of the door.

We're too far gone to stop now, and I'm not walking out of this dressing room until Emma comes.

Keeping my fingers flat on her tongue, I reach around to strum her clit, earning a deep moan around my digits in her mouth.

"Hello?"

The saleslady again.

For fuck's sake.

"We're good, just preparing to come… out shortly. Thank you," I grunt, circling Emma's clit faster, rougher, just the way she likes it.

"Come for me, Emma," I murmur against her ear. "Be a good girl. Look at my dirty little slut stifling her moans in a dressing room while she comes all over my fingers."

Just like that, my words, combined with the rhythm of my fingers on her clit, have her back arching, and she comes, her legs quaking with orgasm. She bites down on my fingers as she rides out her orgasm until her legs actually give out, and I catch her by the waist with a satisfied smile.

She sags against me, her head resting on my shoulder as she tries to catch her breath, sated and sleepy, a blissful smile on her lips.

I press my lips to her head and start to help her with her pants. When we get to the sweater, she tries to pull it over her head, and I stop her.

"Not a chance, Snowflake. I won fair and square. Looks like you're going to be lit *all day* with that sweater on."

"THIS IS EXACTLY WHAT I NEEDED." Emma sighs, taking another sip of her hot chocolate with extra marshmallows, of course. Another thing I learned about her is that if there are sweets involved… she's doubling down. No matter what it is.

"Wanna sit for a minute? Skate time isn't for another…" I

glance down at my watch to check the time. "Thirty minutes."

She nods, and we walk to a table next to the rink that has one of those large commercial heaters above it. While it doesn't completely take the chill away, it's enough to be comfortable and for my fingers to thaw slightly.

When she tries to sit across the table from me, I tug her hand and pull her down onto the seat next to me.

"Sorry, Snowflake. It's cold as hell, and I need all the body heat I can get."

After I just ate her like a starving man in that dressing room, the last thing I want to do is sit *across* from her at a damn table.

"Soo… What's your favorite Christmas candy?" I ask her, scooting slightly closer and tossing my arm casually over the back of the bench.

She drags her fingers along the rim of her hot chocolate for a few seconds before she speaks. "Definitely peppermint bark."

"Peppermint what?"

"You've never had peppermint bark? Oh my God. It's basically the only Christmas treat my mom made growing up, and it's one of my favorites. You take crushed-up peppermints and mix them with white chocolate almond bark, and it's divine. I'm pretty sure it's where my love for sweets started."

"I'll take your word for it. Maybe you can make it for me one day?"

Emma nods. "What about you? What's your favorite?"

"I'm a peanut butter ball kinda guy. My mom makes the best Christmas treats. I always joke that I gain at least fifteen pounds during the holidays because every time I leave her house, I leave with more Tupperware than I can even carry." I laugh. "That's how she is though. We're all grown, and she still cooks us dinner, comes over and does our laundry. Anything to feel close to us, even if we tell her again and again she doesn't have to do any of that stuff. She's the one who plans all of our Christmas festivities. That's why I took on the annual party; she already has enough going on."

Her eyes are soft, and her words are genuine when she says, "She sounds wonderful, Jackson."

"Yeah, she is." I take a sip of my drink. "She's the glue that holds our family together, for sure. So tell me about your family. I, uh, I don't know much about them besides what I've heard throughout the years, and I'd like to hear about them from you."

She blows out a breath before shrugging. "My parents are… very career focused and driven. My dad is an investment banker, and my mom is very into philanthropy. Listening to you talk about your mom and your family… it sounds so different from the way that I grew up. We didn't really have Christmas traditions. I mean, aside from opening presents on Christmas Day and the annual party, there wasn't ever anything that stood out from childhood. We never made cookies or watched the Christmas classics. My parents were just really busy growing up, and I was with my nanny a lot. That's why the party is so important to them—it's the one thing that we really celebrated together. It was always our tradition, and we looked forward to it each year."

I love everything about Christmas with my family, and I hate that she didn't get to do all of those things with hers. But I'm also starting to understand exactly why the party is so important to her and her family. It's their most important tradition.

My gaze softens. "I'm sorry, Emma."

"No, no. You don't have to do that, Jackson. Listen, my parents are wonderful people, and they always provided whatever they could for me. It's just that hearing about your family and your traditions makes me wish that we were able to make more traditions for us. Now, looking back on it as an adult, I feel like while most kids were having snowball fights and building snowmen, I was helping my mom with a party." She laughs. "Completely different Christmas traditions."

"I get it, and I think that just means that you have way more things to experience now. Tell me, have you seen *The Santa Clause*?"

The space between her brow wrinkles as she furrows it. "Is that a movie, or are you talking about the big guy in the red suit?"

"Um, yes. An iconic fucking movie, Snowflake. We've got to rectify this immediately."

She chuckles. "Yeah, I'm pretty sure there are more movies that I haven't seen versus ones that I have."

Reaching out, I slide my palm along hers and lace our fingers together, squeezing gently. "Don't worry, Snowflake. We'll make sure you have some new traditions to add to your list."

12 /

emma

Winter Wonderland

J ackson Pearce is *undeniably* hot.

One look at him, and that much is obvious. Attractive in the way that has your heart hammering in your chest at the very first glance. He's tall and fit with a sharp jaw, warm honey eyes, and a smile that could melt just about anything.

It's part of the reason why staying away from him was so hard in the first place... despite our families' history.

But it's a whole different thing to know that under all of that extremely attractive exterior, he's got a heart to match it.

Something I never expected and never knew until recently. I was perfectly fine having lived my life with all of these assumptions and preconceived notions about him. That he was this frustrating nuisance who just liked to annoy me because of our feuding parties. I was fine hating him because it was what was expected of me.

Until he made it impossible to.

And I don't exactly know what to do with all of these new feelings.

"Admit it, you're having fun." I poke his side as we skate slowly around the rink. Kids are whipping by us at every turn, but I'd like to leave the city without having to visit the ER first, so we're keeping an unhurried pace.

"Only if you admit that wearing ugly sweaters isn't all that bad," he retorts with a smirk.

Exhaling, I roll my eyes playfully. "They're not that bad. Well, I mean, *yours* is absolutely horrific, but still."

His fingers press into my sides unexpectedly, tickling me until I'm breathless and unable to stay on my feet on the slick ice. He sweeps me into his arms to keep me from falling and presses me against the side of the rink.

With the skates on, he's even taller, looming over my small frame, his molten eyes flared with need. "I'm having fun, Snowflake. But I'll be having even more fun later when you're on your knees, when I show you just how much I love when you're a mouthy brat. I'm still thinking about the dressing room. About how tightly your needy pussy squeezed my fingers. I'm about to pop a damn semi in the middle of an ice rink." The deep timbre of his voice in my ear has me pressing my thighs together, my clit now throbbing along with the erratic beat of my heart. He brushes his nose along my jaw in a way that has me shivering, and not at all from the cold.

I'm in danger of doing something insane, like dropping to my knees right in this very spot when someone suddenly crashes into the sideboard right next to us.

"Fuck," Jackson curses and then laughs. "C'mon, let's get out of here."

Not that I needed any convincing, but he takes my hand in his, and together, we skate off the ice to turn in our skates.

After putting our shoes back on and grabbing another hot chocolate for the walk back to the hotel we got in the city, we take the path through the busy park. It's getting dark now, but there are still tons of people out skating, strolling through the park, and some having snowball fights.

I spot a few kids on the ground in the snow-covered grass making snow angels, and I turn to Jackson.

"You know I've never made a snow angel? It seems like something so small and inconsequential, but even as a kid, I never made one."

He stares back at me, blinking, "*Never?*"

"Nope. I'm an only child, Jackson. I never had anyone to play with on snow days."

My gaze drifts back out to the kids rolling around in the fluffy snow until I feel a tug at my hand, and Jackson's taking my hot chocolate and setting it onto a nearby bench alongside his.

"What are you doing?"

"Emma, we're making a fucking snow angel. Right now. You can't live your entire life never having made a snow angel." He's pulling me toward the grass, but I dig my heels in, stopping him.

I shake my head. "I am not lying down in that cold snow! Are you crazy?"

"Yes, we are. You have to."

Clearly, the man has way more strength than I do, not to mention weight and height, so he continues to drag me toward the grass until we're away from everyone else, an undisturbed section of fluffy snowy blanket beneath our feet.

"Jackson, I am not going to get soaking wet—we'll free—"

I don't even get the words out before he's pulling me

down with him, both of us tumbling together into the snow. I land with an oomph on top of him, his body cushioning my fall. Our eyes lock as we breathe heavily, neither of us moving as time seems to still. I can feel this moment in the pounding of my heart, in the fluttering of my pulse. The pull between us.

Then he smiles slyly and pushes me off him onto my back on the snow. "Watch and learn, Snowflake. Watch and learn."

My laugh bubbles out of me as he dramatically moves his arms and legs in a jumping-jack motion, making a snow angel that must be the size of four normal ones.

God, this man.

Emotion creeps its way into my lungs, making it hard for them to expand and even harder for me to control the way my heart thrashes in my chest at the sight of this massive man in the snow, making a snow angel simply because I've never done it before.

He didn't care about the cold or that he would be completely soaked the entire walk back to the hotel because of it. He did it without hesitation, and it makes flurries erupt uncontrollably in my stomach while a realization slams into me full force.

I like Jackson Pearce.

He's kind and compassionate. I like that I can laugh with him and that even the most simple things feel like more fun than I've had in years. He listens to me but also challenges me. Most of all, I feel comfortable around him, and that scares me.

It scares me because it means that these feelings are real, and it's not just physical between us anymore. It feels like more than one heated moment that we gave in to, more than this one day.

"Emma?"

"Hmm?" I say, my gaze on the stars above us.

His gloved hand reaches for me, and then his fingers lace between mine. For a second, we're silent, hand in hand on our backs in the snow, staring up at the inky-black sky dotted with bright stars. Just two snow angels, holding hands.

I feel more at peace than I have in a long time.

"Beautiful," he says, and I nod in agreement.

"Breathtaking."

Except when I glance over, he's not looking at the stars at all. He's looking at *me*.

BACK AT THE HOTEL, after a shower and changing into something warm, I'm bundled up in front of the fire with my notebook and pen. I didn't expect there to be a fireplace in our room, but Jackson upgraded to the executive suite as his way of apologizing for the motel debacle. Even though I told him there was no need to apologize.

We could've booked two rooms, but at this point, I think we've dropped the pretense that we'd be sleeping apart.

"Are you working this late?" Jackson says as he walks up. He's freshly showered and shirtless. My gaze rakes over his muscled torso, drinking in every inch of his chest and abs, down to the pajama bottoms hung low on his hips. His hair is damp and brushed back from his face, and for a moment, I forget what it is I was even working on in the first place until I glance back down at my notebook.

"Yeah, I just wanted to go over a few things for the party. I'm feeling anxious about it."

I honestly haven't even thought about the party for most of the day. I was having so much fun with Jackson that the only thing I could focus on was him. Even now that reality has crept back in, my to-do list feels not quite as important. And that makes me feel like all of my carefully crafted boxes are beginning to crumble little by little. Having things organized and everything going according to plan is the way I keep control of a situation, and right now, I'm beginning to feel that control slipping away. I'm just not ready to admit that out loud to even myself, let alone Jackson.

13 /

emma

The most wonderful time of the year

I can't even believe I'm saying this, but I *miss* Jackson.

I miss his smile, our constant bickering, and the way that he plays with my hair as I fall asleep. I miss how much fun I have when I'm with him. I just miss... *him*.

It's something I never anticipated happening. Lately, I feel like I say that all the time.

It's barely been twenty-four hours since we returned home from the city, back to real life, since we left behind the bubble we found ourselves in while away from Strawberry Hollow.

We're back to where he can't just grab my hand as we walk on the street because the entire town would see. God, I can't even tell my best friend, Katie, about this because I don't know what "*this*" even is.

We got stuck together planning this party, then had incredible sex that led to even more incredible sex.

But the two days we spent together felt like *more* than just sex.

It feels like he's slowly sneaking inside my heart, and I'm scared to think about what that could *actually* mean.

In the twenty-four hours since we got home, he's crossed my mind more times than I want to count, definitely more times than I want to admit.

We've checked a lot off our list, and while there are plenty of things still for us to do to prepare for the party, it's now mostly things we can each handle on our own.

Groaning, I drop my head back on the couch, clutching the wineglass in my hand a little tighter, praying the red merlot inside doesn't splash onto the floor. It's not my first glass of the night because I just spent the weekend locked away with the sexiest man in town and his wicked tongue, with a body straight from the heavens. A man whom I might actually be starting to have *real* feelings for, but, oh wait, our families have been feuding for decades, and we were basically born hating each other.

Everything's just great over here.

My phone buzzes on the armchair of the couch, and I pick it up as I take another hefty swig of my merlot.

Mother: How is the party planning going? Your father is not taking it well, but that was to be expected. I'm trying to do damage control, but you know how he is when it comes to the Pearce family. He's planning on anchoring the decorations in the ground because of last year's debacle.

Yes, well, at least someone in our family still dislikes the Pearce family because I, for one, think I actually might be falling for one, and I already know that the outcome is going to be a disaster.

Me: It's going well. Everything should go off without a hitch.

As soon as I press Send, the doorbell rings, and I sigh wearily.

Probably carolers, if I had to guess. Obviously, not my parents since my mom is currently texting me, and she rarely steps foot in my house. So, I'm not sure who else would be stopping by this late.

I set my phone down on the end table and walk to the front door, opening it with one hand while holding my wine in the other.

I was absolutely *not* prepared for who I'd find on the other side, my eyes widening in surprise.

"Jackson?"

He grins. "Hey, Snowflake."

I don't even bother correcting him because I'm too busy checking him out. He's wearing a black hoodie with a pair of dark gray sweatpants.

Ugh, he's exactly the reason that gray sweatpants are the equivalent of porn for women. I can practically see the outline of his dick just staring at me. I need more wine.

"Let me get in the door first, woman. Jeez, I can feel you undressing me with those eyes," he teases.

"I'm sorry! I just couldn't contain myself," I respond, rolling my eyes but stifling a giggle. "You and that ego. But okay, fine, I was admiring your gray sweatpants era."

Only then do I realize he's got his hands full of stuff, and immediately, my hosting persona kicks in.

Way to leave him out on the doorstep in the cold, Emma.

"Crap, come in, come in, sorry!" I squeak, opening the door wider with my foot.

Jackson steps inside and glances around the entryway into

the living room, his jaw agape. "Emma Worthington, you've been holding back on me."

Well, maybe a *little*…

I shrug, turning toward my living room, which is the epitome of cozy. Growing up, our house was beautiful. Grand staircase, marble floors, expensive art throughout the house. Beautiful, but… kind of cold. There were never any photos on the wall except, of course, the family portrait that hung in the dining room. No personal touches.

I always knew I wanted my home to be the opposite, less curated and more warm, so I may have gone just a tad bit… overboard?

With Christmas decorations.

My tree is massive, taking up the whole far corner of my living room. It's decorated in traditional red and green with pops of gold and white throughout, with a vintage red Christmas train wrapped around its base and a custom-made star at the top. The fireplace mantel is covered with a fir garland, mismatched hand-knitted stockings, and tons of nutcrackers I've collected over the years. My windows are all covered with twinkle lights, my couch is covered in festive reindeer pillows, and my entry table displays my beloved Christmas village, complete with little villager figurines that I've collected throughout the years. It's truly my most prized possession.

And that's just my living room.

Almost every single surface of my house has some type of decoration on it, and I love it. It feels like *home*. My safe place to land.

"Yes, well, you never asked," I retort, hiding my smile

behind the rim of my wineglass as I take a sip. "So, are we having surprise visits now?"

We walk to the kitchen. He sets down the six-pack of beer and the paper bag and shrugs, "Guess I kind of missed you insulting me."

"Guess I kind of missed insulting you."

His eyes dance with amusement. "Well, good thing I'm here, then. Figured I'd come by and make you watch a Christmas movie with me. Unless you've got some other important plans?"

I glance down at my attire, a pair of old sweatpants with little Rudolphs on them and an old baggy T-shirt from high school. My hair is practically a rat's nest, and I have zero makeup on.

"Oh, I was just heading out for drinks. Can't you tell by this outfit?" I laugh. "I look like I just crawled out of bed."

"You look sexy in anything," he says, stepping closer and taking the wineglass out of my hand, then carefully setting it onto the island beside us. "And I fucking missed you, Emma."

My heart pounds in my chest as I nod. "I missed you too."

Jackson slides his hands along my jaw, cradling it as he lowers his lips to mine, kissing me as if he hasn't seen me in days when it's only been twenty-four hours.

Part of me wants to tell him that we should stop, that we should quit while we still can, that this was just a weekend fling. But an even bigger part of me knows that it would be pointless because my heart is already involved.

He pulls back slightly, ghosting his thumb along my jaw as he stares into my eyes. It feels... overwhelming and amazing to have a man look at you the way that Jackson is looking at me right now. But also terrifying because I have no idea what the future holds for us.

Our families have hated each other since before we were born, and I just don't think it's possible for them to even be *civil*, let alone get along.

"So, movies?" I say, clearing my throat. "Do I get to pick?"

"Yep."

Jackson grabs a beer, and I refill my wine before we walk back to the living room and take a seat on the plush couch.

"Okay, what about *Elf*?" he says, grabbing the remote and pulling me toward him until I'm partially on top of him, tucked against his side.

He does it naturally, without hesitation, and it makes my heart race.

Being with Jackson feels… like something that I should've always done.

It feels right.

"A classic, for sure," I say. "Let's do it."

A second later, *Elf* appears on the screen, and I burrow into Jackson's side, and we spend the next few hours watching a few of the classics I never got to see growing up.

It's late, well after 2:00 a.m., if I had to guess, when Jackson stretches beneath me, a deep groan rumbling from his chest. I dozed off sometime during the third movie, and now I'm entirely too comfortable to move.

"I need to go."

His words are whispered against my ear, and I moan sleepily. "You could… stay?"

"As much as I want to, if I do, someone's going to see Pearce Builders parked outside your house in the morning, and the entire town will know before noon."

As much as I don't want him to go, he's right. It's enough that the entire town is gossiping about the two of us spending time together to plan the party. Imagine if they knew what was *actually* happening.

"Okay, okay." I groan as I lift myself off him, but he stops me, grabbing my chin between his fingers. Only then do I shake off the grogginess of sleep and open my eyes to stare into his warm, whiskey irises.

"Trust me, Emma, there is nothing more that I want than to wake up with you in my arms. It's all I fucking want. I just don't want to make any more gossip than there already is. To do anything that will stress you more. You can't blink in this town without everyone knowing, you know that," he says, brushing my hair back out of my face.

I nod. "I know. I understand."

"But I've been thinking about this since we were in the city…" he starts, stopping to brush his finger along my bottom lip. "I don't… want this to stop. Seeing you. Kissing you. Being with you."

"I don't want that either," I say honestly. I wasn't sure how he felt about whatever this is between us, but relief floods my chest at his admission. It's nice to know that he feels the same way.

"Let's take it one day at a time? We have this party—let's just get through that, and then we can focus on what's between us. In the meantime, we'll keep things quiet. We'll figure it out, Emma," he says confidently, and I nod in agreement.

One day at a time.

Easier said than done.

14 /
emma

The Art of Decorating

"Okay, a little to the left. Yes, maybe like an inch? A *liiiittle* more," I say, squinting as Jackson moves the garland over two inches to the left. Crap, now it looks slightly off center. "Wait, that's too far."

He groans. "Woman, I barely moved the damn thing."

"Well, you barely moved it just a little too far."

We've been at Town Hall all morning, putting up decorations, setting up the tables, organizing everything that's finally been delivered. The party is only a few days away, and I'm starting to panic… slightly. Even my to-do list isn't keeping my anxiety under control.

It's Jackson who's somehow managing to keep my head on my shoulders with reassuring words and gentle reminders to give myself grace. Not even a month ago, we were publicly wrestling over a nutcracker, and now *he's* the one keeping me calm.

"You know," he says, climbing down from the new ladder I made him purchase from the hardware store so there wouldn't be a repeat of the last time we were here and he almost died. "I think you just like to stare at my ass while I'm on this ladder, moving shit around."

I can't stop the smile that flits to my lips at his teasing, maybe because he might be partially right. Just a *tad*.

I mean… it *is* a very nice ass.

An ass that was *made* for Wranglers.

Honestly, who would've thought I would be so attracted to a man who wears nothing but old jeans and worn boots?

"I fucking love when you do that," he murmurs as he closes the distance between us and slides his calloused hand into the hair at my nape.

"Do what?"

The corner of his lip tugs up. "When your cheeks flush pink, and your eyes get hazy and unfocused, I know you're thinking of something that has you blushing… like my cock."

"Can you be so sure that it's *your* cock I'm thinking about?" I tease.

A low, growly noise leaves his throat, and I squeak when he leans forward and nips at my bottom lip with his teeth. "Better fucking be my cock, Snowflake. Not sure if you've gathered yet, but I'm not interested in sharing."

Apparently, he likes to play with fire almost as much as I like to stoke it, so I lean forward, gently brushing my lips along his until his hand tightens in the hair at my nape. "But that would have to mean that I was already yours, Jackson Pearce."

His eyes flare with possessiveness. But just as he opens his mouth to respond, the front door of Town Hall is wrenched open suddenly, and we break apart like we're two guilty teenagers who've just been caught making out in a closet.

And I guess... with the sneaking around we've been doing this week, we kind of are.

Mayor Davis steps through the door with a wide smile and a bright red Santa hat that matches his cheeks. "Ah, just the two that I wanted to see!"

Jackson coughs, clearing his throat, and I'm pretty sure my heart is at the bottom of my stomach from almost getting caught. I was two seconds away from dropping to my knees and showing Jackson just how much I really *was* thinking about his cock.

"Hi, Mr. Davis!" I squeak as I begin to busy myself with stuffing the napkins into the holders, completely avoiding his gaze.

Thankfully, Jackson is more smooth than I am and takes charge. He walks over to Mayor Davis and shakes his hand. "Mornin', Jed. Come to check on your favorite criminals?"

He chuckles. "It's a tough job! Someone's gotta do it. Just wanted to drop by and see how everything is coming along?"

"Oh... it's a-comin'," Jackson replies, and I all but choke on my own spit. *Saint Nick on a sleigh.* "We're practically coming all the time. You know... to Town Hall to get things done."

His eyes flit to mine, and he winks, then tells Mayor Davis to follow him to the other side of the building to show off his handiwork in getting the twelve-foot tree up this morning.

He's completely lost his mind.

While Jackson's showing Mayor Davis our work in progress, I spend the next few minutes working on the napkins, then begin setting out the place cards. I fought hard for these, but in the end, turns out I can get Jackson to agree to *practically* anything when my mouth is involved.

A very helpful tool that I plan to keep in my back pocket for the foreseeable future when I'm not in the mood to compromise.

Checking my to-do list, I make a quick note to order a new dress for the party. I have options, but… I want to order something I know that is going to really wow this year, and I don't think I have anything in my closet that can accomplish that.

"Everything's looking wonderful, Emma!" Mayor Davis suddenly says behind me, causing me to jump. I turn to face him, pasting on a smile.

"Thank you. We've been working really hard to have everything done in time and to make sure it's a great party for all of Strawberry Hollow."

He nods. "You can absolutely tell. Wonderful. You know, I wasn't one hundred percent convinced the two of you were going to be able to pull this off. Wayne had his doubts —heck, most of the town has doubts—but I am very pleased to see that everything is going right as rain and you're working together. It's good to see you burying the hatchet."

"Yep, we're burying it for sure. *Very deep.*" Jackson gives a self-satisfied smirk, crossing his arms over his chest.

Before that, I was two seconds away from throttling him with a festive napkin holder, but now I'm distracted by his perfect forearms.

And that's how I got myself into this situation in the first place.

Lusting over Jackson Pearce and his stupid, muscled, veiny, sexy-as-hell arms.

Damn arm porn.

"Yes, well, we of course have been putting our differences aside for the sake of planning the party," I say.

"Very good, very good. Well, I'll get out of your hair and allow you to continue the amazing work you're doing here. I'm looking forward to the big event."

Smiling, I nod and narrow my gaze at Jackson, who is trying his damnedest not to laugh.

He shakes the mayor's hand again, and then together, we watch him walk back out of the door, leaving us alone.

"I'm going to kill you!" I screech, rushing over to slap his arm, but he catches my hand in his and pulls me to him, sealing his lips over mine.

"I've been dying to kiss you since the moment he walked in that damn door, Snowflake. Hush," he whispers against my lips, nibbling on my lip before teasing the seam of them with his tongue. "You make me fucking crazy, you know that?"

"The feeling is mutual. God, I can't believe you said that to him. What if he suspects something is going on with us?" This time, I do playfully hit his chest, and he only grins harder.

His shoulder dips in a shrug. "He doesn't have a clue. He's just happy that the two of us haven't killed each other and he doesn't have to lock us back up in jail to give us a stern talking-to."

True.

But still...

"We already have almost every single eye in the town on us, Jackson. We have to be careful that this doesn't blow up in our faces and cause a huge stink before we can pull this party off."

"I know," he sighs heavily, pressing his lips to mine again. "How's your to-do list looking? Got everything checked off for the day?"

The way he says it, in a way that's not poking fun at my list like he used to, makes the flurries in my stomach flip. He understands now that being organized to have everything go as planned is part of who I am.

"Yes. The cake will be delivered the night before, and we're going to store it in the fridge at Mimi's bakery. She said with it being so close to Christmas, she has the room with all of her orders already being delivered. The band will be here an hour before to set up, and as requested, classics only. But I did ask for a set list just to go over and make sure it's all approved." I step back and walk over to my to-do list and pick it and my pen up, my eyes scanning the neat black ink on the notebook paper.

"Of course you did, Snowflake. What about the caterers?"

I look for the section on catering and tap it with the end of my pen. "All squared away. I gave them our selections off their premade menu, and they'll be here early to set up as well."

"Well, it looks like all we've really got left is to make sure the decorations are exactly the way you like them... and to make sure our families survive the night without a Christmas brawl." He laughs, dragging a hand through his hair.

He's joking, but... it's not out of the realm of possibilities. Not that a Worthington would *ever*, but I don't put it past my father to have a few choice words after a few drinks.

I just need this to go off without a hitch, for it to be done so I don't have to stress about it any longer, so I can spend the rest of the holidays doing all of the things that I love when it comes to Christmas. Knitting Christmas socks, spending nights by the fire with a mug of hot chocolate, and especially going to the tree lighting in Town Square.

"I can practically see the wheels turning in here," Jackson says, tapping my temple lightly. "You okay?"

I nod. "Yes. Just... ready for it to be over, as sad as that sounds."

"It's a lot of pressure, but remember... it's what I'm here for, Snowflake. If you need to offload something onto me, do it, and don't think twice about it. We're both responsible for this, so you don't have to do all the work."

"Thank you." Rising onto my toes, I press a gentle kiss to the corner of his mouth and slide my hands from his chest up to grasp behind his neck.

"I'm not sure if this is the right time to ask, but I'd like for you to spend the night with me at my place tomorrow night. And, uh, my family has dinner every other week, and I wanted you to go with me."

"Yeah, right." I laugh incredulously. "You're hilarious."

"I'm serious, Emma. I want to bring you with me. Look, we both know our families have... their issues, but I want you to meet them knowing what you know now. I've already talked to my mom, and she's excited to meet you."

This is a big step. Actually, not even a step at all—this is walking right off the side of a cliff.

It's practically walking into a room full of people who already think you're terrible. Who think your whole family is terrible... and have for years.

There's no way this will go well.

"Please, Snowflake? I want you to get to know them, and them to know you the way that I have. I promise you my family would never be rude to you or disrespect you in any way. I would never allow that. It would mean a lot to me if you came. We're going to do our annual gingerbread house competition, and I need all the help I can get. I'll even let you be in charge of decorations. I know that gets you hot," he teases with a wink.

Tossing my head back, I laugh, cursing away my watery eyes. I can't resist him when he's being flirty... and truthfully, I am kind of curious to see a different side to his family, like I have with him. "Fine. But I still think it's going to be an absolute disaster."

"Never. You'll see. Meet me at my house at five? I promise at any time if you feel uncomfortable or want to leave, then we'll leave, no questions asked... I'll even let you drive us in your fancy car."

"Okay, I'll come. But... what should I even wear?"

Jackson laughs. "*Definitely* the ugly sweater I defiled you in, Snowflake."

15 /
jackson
Christmas Spirit-ish

Unsurprisingly, Emma's early.

I hear her car pull down the drive at ten till five, and of course, both Marley and Mo lose it the second I open the front door, booking it down the steps to her car before she can even kill the engine. Clearly, I'm not the only one who loves having Emma around. Those two are as taken with her as I am, and it's just another thing I love about her.

She's only met them a few times, but even when they jump up on her in excitement, she treats them lovingly, like they're family, not like the wild nuisances most people see them as. A man can tell a lot about a woman by the way she treats his dogs.

Leaning against the porch rail, I watch as she immediately drops her bag and squats so she can give them both head scratches. She doesn't even flinch as they undoubtedly leave her covered in puppy slobber and fur.

This girl is working her way into my heart, and I'm not sure that I want to stop her.

"Hiya, handsome," she says as she walks up the steps, Mo and Marley flanking each side, the lights on her sweater blinking.

"Can't believe you actually wore it, Snowflake. I'm impressed." Reaching for her, I take the overnight bag off her shoulder and sling it over mine before pulling her to me, capturing her lips. "Even sexier than last time. Although, I think once we get home, we need a repeat of the dressing room."

She hums against my lips, her fingers tangling into the front of my shirt. "Wait." Pulling back, she rakes her eyes down my shirt, a frown forming on her lips. "Jackson Pearce, you better go right back into that house and put on your ugly sweater, or I am *not* going! You can't expect me to be the only one to wear one!"

I was wondering how long it would take her to realize that I didn't have mine on.

"How about you let me take yours off before we go? Damn, Snowflake, I love it when you're feisty." I waggle my brows, and she rolls her eyes, stepping around me and through the front door.

"Let me guess, that's why you love to push my buttons so badly? C'mon, Mar, Mo! We're leaving your daddy out here to *freeze*."

And to absolutely no one's surprise, the little heathen traitors march right past me and follow her into the house, leaving my ass out in the cold.

After getting the dogs situated, my house locked up, and Emma in the car, we make a short drive over to my parents' house and park in the driveway. I walk around the truck and open Emma's door, sliding my hand into hers as I help her out.

"Don't be nervous," I tell her, shutting the door behind her, and we make our way up the sidewalk.

"I'm not nervous," she says too quickly, avoiding my eyes.

She's *absolutely* fucking nervous. Since I've gotten to know her a bit better, I know that's not a feeling that Emma likes to experience, so I want to calm her where I can.

I stop her before we reach the steps, turning her to face me as I grasp her chin between my fingers, tilting it up. "Okay, maybe you're not nervous. Maybe you are and don't want to admit it. Either way, I'll be here. I promise it'll be fine. My parents will love you once they get to know you. It's just dinner, nothing fancy." Reaching between us, I grab her fingers, which were fidgeting with the hem of her sweater, and lace them between mine, squeezing gently. "C'mon, Snowflake."

After a few beats, she nods, exhaling, "Okay. Let's do this."

Before we can even make it to the front door, it swings open and Ma steps out, a bright smile on her face. "There you two are! We were about to get started without you."

I can feel Emma tense beside me, her fingers gripping mine tightly before she lifts her other gloved hand to wave at Ma.

My mom is the kind of woman who has never once met a stranger. Anywhere we go, she's making conversation with people she's never met like she's known them for years. The grocery store, the post office, the hardware store—hell, she'd pick up hitchhikers on the side of the damn road if my dad wouldn't keel over from a heart attack.

So it doesn't surprise me in the least that she walks directly to Emma and pulls her into one of her big hugs, patting her back gently as she whispers against her ear, "Hi, Emma. I'm Lucy, and I am so excited to have you here tonight."

Emma quickly recovers from the initial shock and returns her hug. "Thank you so much for having me," she says sincerely.

Ma pulls back from Emma and tosses me a wink before giving me a tight hug. She glances back at Emma. "Oh, I just *love* your sweater!"

"Ah, oh, yes, this sweater is one hundred percent your son's doing." Emma glances down at her sweater and then back at Ma. "He seems to have me doing all the crazy things this year."

A grin forms on my lips, watching the exchange between the woman I love the most and a girl who I never expected to want to be around who's suddenly the *only* one I want to be around. The one who's invaded my thoughts and my heart. I fucking love seeing them together.

"Well, y'all come on in. It's freezing out here, and we've got a whole house full of people who want to officially meet you." Ma links her arm in Emma's and pats it gently. "Now, you don't let those boys bother you, Emma. They're going to poke fun, I'm sure, but if any one of them steps out of line, they know they're never too old for my wooden spoon."

Emma chuckles, nodding. "Yes, ma'am."

I'm thankful that Ma stepped up before we got inside to ease her nerves a little because Lord knows the second we walk over the threshold, it's going to be absolute, pure chaos.

When we walk in, my little sister, Josie, is currently sitting on our oldest brother Jensen's shoulders, swaying as she tries to put the star on the top of the tree. She looks like she's about two seconds from falling off his shoulders, but you'd never know it by the way she's laughing and yanking at his hair with one hand.

Welcome to the Pearce family.

"Oh, Josie, be careful! You do know we have a ladder?" Ma says, shaking her head with a wry grin. "I am not going to Dr. Grant tonight for stitches or a concussion."

"We're fine, Ma!" Jensen quips. "She weighs a hundred pounds soaking wet."

"Hey!" Josie says, bopping him on top of the head. "One twenty-five, thank you *very* much."

I just shake my head and walk into the kitchen behind Ma and Emma. This was my favorite place in our house growing up. It's where we ate dinner together every night. Where we had family meetings, did projects, spent late nights on homework. Where we decorated cookies with Ma every Christmas as we drank hot cocoa and listened to her favorite holiday music. It's the one place in the house where you'd always find one of us. The table where my dad and my other brothers, Jude and Jameson, are currently sitting is the same table that was here when I was a kid.

"Wow, look what the cat dragged in," Jude drawls. "Oh, but he brought a friend." Standing from his chair, he walks over to Emma and offers his hand. "I don't think we've ever *officially* met. Just kind of… seen each other from a distance. I'm Jude, this shithead's little brother. Also, the most attractive of all the Pearce brothers… obviously."

Her brow arches. "*Obviously*," she says with humor.

That earns him a slap to the back of the head from me. "Watch it, asshole."

Emma better think that *I* am the most attractive Pearce. Though, hell, if you put the four of us together in a line, it's probably hard to tell us apart. The Pearce genes run strong.

"What? She agrees! I can't help it if I'm the best-looking." He shrugs.

Ignoring him, I lace my fingers back in Emma's to pull her toward me and away from my brother, then walk to my dad and Jameson to make the introductions.

"Hi, Emma." Dad smiles warmly, shaking her hand.

Jameson's... being fucking Jameson. He simply gives her a nod.

It has nothing to do with her and everything to do with the fact that he's a grumpy fuck, but I narrow my gaze at him anyway, warning him to behave.

"Emma, honey, wanna help me with these meat pies?" Ma asks from the kitchen island.

"Yes, of course." She squeezes my hand lightly, then lets go and walks across the kitchen to where my mom is working on finishing supper.

Josie walks through the door at the same time I pull out a chair at the kitchen table and sit next to Dad. I watch as she introduces herself, and then they start talking about Emma's sweater, which quickly shifts into talking about holiday decor.

"I totally knew you were an interior designer. I'm so excited you love Pottery Barn as much as I do! I feel like their Christmas decorations are so nostalgic. They take me back to when I was a kid," Josie says, dreamily sighing.

Emma nods. "Yes! I love the classic look. Wait, please tell me you're a fan of their classic knit?"

"Duh!" Josie responds excitedly, and that's where I zone out because I have no idea what the fuck "classic knit" is. But I'm relieved that the conversation between them seems easy, like they've been friends all their life, not like we're two families who have spent years feuding.

A stupid feud if you ask me. Especially now that I know Emma like I do.

"You sure you know what you're doing, brother? A *Worthington* of all people?" Jude says quietly, nodding at Emma.

For a second, I'm silent as I think of what to say, my jaw working in the process. I hate the way he even says her last name like an *insult*. Part of me wants to tell him to fuck off, even if he is my brother, but then I remember... this is how it's always been for our families, the feud drawing a line clear down the center of our town with us on one side and them on the other. And they haven't gotten to know her how I have yet. Truth is, we've barely ever even talked to the Worthingtons, so how could they really know her?

"Yeah, I do," I say simply. Because that's the thing—as close as I am to my family, I don't *owe* them or *anyone* an explanation about what's happening between Emma and me. Whatever we decide, whatever happens between us, is just that—between us.

"She's nothing like I thought. You know, I've spent my entire life judging her based on the stupid feud between our families, thinking that I knew *exactly* who she was. And I was dead fucking wrong, Jude. She's smart and passionate. Ambitious. Fun. She makes me laugh. She gives me shit just as hard as I give it to her. Matches me toe to toe."

Jude nods as his shoulder dips. "Maybe we have misjudged her, but honestly, can you blame us? Look at the shit her family has done over the years. It's hard to just... forget all that."

"And the shit *we've* done? Look, I'm not asking everyone to forget what's happened. I'm asking my family to understand that I *see* this girl, and I need y'all to give her a chance. To try to see what I see. And to recognize that neither of our families are innocent in this. I know that you're defensive because we're protective of Ma—I get it. But Emma deserves to be seen for who she really is and not just what this feud has made her seem like."

I can see the mistrust shining in his eyes as he sits silently. Jude's always been the fiercely protective brother, even being the youngest, so I knew he'd have something to say about me bringing Emma home.

"I might not trust her... yet. But I trust you. Trust your judgment. If you know what you're doing, then I trust that. I'll give her a chance."

I nod. "That's all I ask."

Jude nods, and the conversation shifts, Dad asking about the upcoming projects we've got scheduled for the new year, and I go back to watching Emma interacting with Ma and Josie, unable to keep the smile off my face. Ma is showing them how she makes my favorite dessert, peanut butter balls, and she's watching intently while Josie keeps sneaking bites of peanut butter when no one is looking.

When she realizes she's been caught, she winks, shoveling another chocolate-covered ball into her mouth.

I somehow drag my gaze away and try to refocus on the conversation with Dad and Jude until Emma joins me at the table with a casserole dish, followed by Ma, Jensen, and Josie.

It feels like it always does, coming home.

Chaotic, but also full of happiness and love. In everything we do.

Except this time, I've got Emma with me. I wondered what it would be like having her here with my family, and all I can think about is how much I love it.

I know that sounds crazy, but things are changing between us. She's letting down her walls, letting me in, and now that I know her, I can never go back to how things were before this. It's impossible, not when she's shown me who she *really* is.

Everyone makes a plate, and we talk about our days, what's been happening with everybody since last dinner, and, of course, the party comes up.

"So, how's the party planning going?" Josie asks, her brown eyes dancing with amusement. "You two are the only thing the town's been talking about."

Emma slants her gaze at me, then clears her throat and looks back at Josie. "It's going really well. We're making good progress, and I think everything will go as planned. Well, hopefully."

"It will," I say, reaching next to me beneath the table to squeeze her hand. "Emma's amazing at all of this. She's the one who's planned everything and has made sure it's gone smoothly so far. I'm just the muscles behind the show."

Jensen chuckles. "Yeah, well, you two managing to get our families together under one roof for the first time probably ever is the equivalent of hell freezing over, so…"

My gaze narrows, and he shrugs. "What? It's true. You can't expect us to pretend like the feud doesn't exist simply because you're bringing the enemy home. You know how snobby they've been to us."

"Jensen, enough!" Ma chides. "We will not have you being rude to guests."

Dad nods. "And we've already discussed that everyone is going to be on their best behavior this year, so watch it. Emma is here as your brother's guest, and we're not going to make her uncomfortable." He eyes each of my brothers and even Josie, who just rolls her eyes.

"Dad, get real. *Most* of us can act like adults." She sticks her tongue out at Jensen and then winks at Emma.

"I know, which is why I want to be very clear that although we may not always get along with the Worthingtons —" He tosses Emma a glance and winces. "Well, previously, we have all had many… moments of contention…but we're all going to try and move past that. Right, Lucy?"

Ma nods, her expression softening when she looks at Emma. "Absolutely. Emma, honey, you are welcome at our home anytime. I hope you know that."

"Thank you. All of you, for being so kind to me. I-I wasn't sure what to expect," Emma says. "I know that our families have always… had animosity, but I'm hoping that this could be an olive branch between us? I can't speak for my parents, but I can speak for myself."

Her hand squeezes mine, and I glance over, wishing that I could drag her out of that damn chair and kiss her in front of everyone.

"You can *always* expect to find kindness in our home, Emma. We're happy you're here. And if my boys give you any trouble, you let me know, and I'll keep them in line. Sometimes they don't think with their heads," my dad says to her, and she nods.

When she turns to look at me and I see that her eyes are watery, I clear my throat and change the subject to something a little lighter. "So… how about those gingerbread houses?"

16 /
emma

Naughty... or nice?

I truly had no idea what I was going to be walking into when I agreed to go to Jackson's parents' for dinner. I guess maybe I expected there to be, at the very least, awkward, uncomfortable silence? Maybe even someone making offhand comments. It's probably what would have happened if the tables were turned and we went to my house for dinner.

But that's not at all how tonight has gone.

Sure, his brother made a snarky comment, but honestly, I probably deserved it with how my family and I behaved in the past.

"Snowflake, I'm sorry, but that looks terrible," Jackson mutters teasingly from behind me. "I *think* I might have made a mistake asking you to be on my team."

I whip around to face him, my lips twisted in a scowl. "That is *very* rude. It's just… a work in progress. Trust the process, Jackson Pearce."

Okay, maybe… I'm lying.

There is absolutely no saving this thing. The icing is

sliding off the sides, the gumdrops are swallowed inside it somewhere, and the roof is completely crooked, but you know what? A for effort on my very first gingerbread house.

It doesn't help that Jude, Jackson's younger brother, has been making me laugh the entire time. I'm... distracted.

And speaking of, what has *Jackson* actually done to further this gingerbread house along? The answer is nothing. He's been staring at my ass while I bent over the table, sneaking small touches for the past twenty minutes. The man is in construction, for fuck's sake! He should be nailing this, but he's clearly too busy checking me out instead. And... I don't hate it.

"We're gonna have to do a few practice runs for next year," he teases. "Make sure we're prepared to win."

My heart flutters at the mention of next year, as if it's already a done thing that I'm going to be a part of his family's Christmas traditions.

True to his word, he's hardly left my side all night, and it's been reassuring. Even though I didn't need it as much as I thought I would, it's nice to know that he wasn't just ready to throw me to the wolves.

"Do y'all remember a few years ago when we had so many damn lights at the party that we blew the electricity all the way to Evergreen Lane?" Jensen stops working on his much better-looking gingerbread house to address the table.

My eyes widen. "Oh God, I do remember that! My parents were so mad because of course our party was on the same night, and we were without power for so long that we had to end the party early and send everyone home. We didn't even get to finish dinner."

Jensen nods with a smirk, and Jude elbows him as if to tell him to shut up.

"It's okay," I tell him, a soft smile on my lips. "It's kind of the... elephant in the room, and like we said, we can't pretend it doesn't exist. It's in the past, right?"

Everyone nods, and Jackson steps closer behind me, wrapping his arm around my waist protectively, stirring something in my chest.

It's sweet that he's going out of his way to make me feel comfortable and secure.

"Yeah. The funny part was, I'm pretty sure I have *never* seen Wayne's face turn that red. I thought for sure he'd have a heart attack when we had to call the main power station to send someone out," Josie adds, her dark hair swaying as she throws her head back in laughter. "That's saying a lot because remember the year before when Jameson got shitfaced at the party, and you guys bet him five hundred bucks he wouldn't ride the sleigh into town with Albert?"

My brow furrows. Albert...?

"My parents' mule." Jackson's breath is hot against my neck as he clues me in.

I can practically picture his brother in a life-size red sleigh with a donkey pulling it, going at a turtle's pace all the way into town.

"But he did, and guess what?" Josie says, looking pointedly at Jameson. "He did it in his *underwear*. Wayne loved that one. Both Mom and Dad had to go get him downtown because they were going to book him."

Yawning, I set the bag of icing down on the table and then pull out my phone to check the time.

10:45.

I didn't realize how quickly time had flown in between dinner and the gingerbread houses.

"You tired, Snowflake?" Jackson asks, tightening his arm around my waist.

I nod. "Yeah, I didn't sleep well last night… I think I was just nervous?"

"C'mon, let's get out of here. Pretty sure we're not even in the *realm* of winning this thing, and I can't fucking wait to get you home."

Not that I expected to with the disaster that was our Pearce Family Gingerbread Contest entry.

His mom and sister pull me in for a hug, telling me to come back anytime and that they loved having me. It makes me feel so much better, knowing that my nerves were for nothing.

They didn't have to accept me with open arms, but they did, and I'm so thankful that I came.

It's one giant step in the right direction. To *finally* put this feud behind us.

ONCE WE'RE BACK at Jackson's house and he brings my bags to the bedroom, he says as he leans against the doorframe, "I'm going to lock the house up. Bathroom's right there. Be back in a few."

His bedroom is exactly as I would've imagined. Dark wood paired with gray and black throughout. Masculine, neat, and simple. Just the way that he is.

The bed is neatly made, and there are piles of pillows that I absolutely can't wait to sink into.

Slipping my toiletry bag from my overnight bag, I walk to the bathroom to quickly get ready for bed. After brushing my teeth, washing my face, and pulling my long hair up in a bun, I walk back into his bedroom, where he's sitting on the edge of his bed, scrolling on his phone.

"Oh! I almost forgot," I say, dropping my toiletry bag back into my overnight bag. "I have something for you."

"Is it lingerie? I knew I was going to get my Christmas wish, Emma."

Laughing, I pull out the matching red outfits I knitted. "Well... it is clothing. Sort of. I made Marley and Mo *matching* Christmas sweaters."

I realize that it's probably kind of silly to make his dogs Christmas sweaters, but I figured if we have ugly sweaters, then they should too.

"You knitted those... *for my dogs*?" His brow lifts in surprise, and an expression I can't quite read passes over his face.

I nod. "I know... it's kind of silly, but I just th—"

The words die on my lips as he crosses the room, grabbing my face and slanting his lips over mine, moving them in a kiss that is so powerful, so intense, so purposeful that it feels like my knees might actually give out.

"You are fucking perfect, Emma Worthington, and I was a fool for ever thinking you were anything other than that," he says, dropping his forehead against mine.

My heart is pounding inside my chest so hard it feels like it might burst through.

"It's just sweaters, Jackson," I whisper quietly. "I just wanted them to have something festive too."

He shakes his head. "It's *not* just a sweater, Emma. It's everything." Holding my jaw in his hands, he leans in and kisses me tenderly, with barely a brush of his lips across mine, then sighs. "I don't want this to end. I don't want to walk away from you."

"Then don't," I say, rising onto my toes to meet his lips. "For the first time in my life, I'm doing something for *me*, without the scrutiny or expectations of anyone else. And I want *you*, Jackson Pearce. Even if we have no idea what the future holds or how we're going to make this work with our family issues. For once, I'm not going to plan for something to go wrong or try to control everything. I'm going to follow my heart and hope that it's not going to steer me wrong."

Jackson's throat bobs as he swallows, his pupils turning into molten chocolate as they darken. "I won't hurt you."

I nod. "I trust you. With my body. With my heart. Especially with my heart."

In a blink, he's sweeping me off my feet and carrying me to his bed, laying me down on the plush comforter as he hovers over me. "Then, let me show you how I'll take care of you, Emma."

He leans forward and claims my mouth with gentle reverence, licking at the seam of my lips as he delves into my mouth, our tongues tangling together and leaving me a breathless mess beneath him. I've never been treated with such... *care.*

Our eyes lock, and my head feels dizzy from the intensity of his gaze, like he's seeing inside of me and chipping away at any obstacles left between us. The rough, calloused pads of his fingers dance along the hem of my sweater, and soon, he's peeling it off, then tossing it off the bed.

His eyes rake down my body as he leans forward and pulls down the cups of my bra, latching onto my nipple with a rough suck, causing me to cry out at the sensation.

Everything feels hypersensitive tonight.

My body is a live wire that responds to his touch in a powerful, out-of-body experience.

Maybe it's because we're not just using our bodies but because now our hearts are clearly involved.

"So goddamn beautiful," he says through a heavy-lidded stare. "I want to fuck these, mark them, make you fucking mine, Snowflake."

God, this man is superior at being inherently filthy, and my clit throbs in response to each syllable as he speaks.

"It's like you were made for me. Every inch of you was made to bring me to my knees, Emma."

My hands slide around his nape, yanking him down to my lips as I kiss him with urgency, our tongues frantically battling together. I slide my hands beneath his sweater, along the rigid expanse of his abs, and then, because I know how much he loves it, I drag my nails lightly down the muscles there, earning me a guttural groan that rumbles from deep in his chest.

When he reaches behind his neck to pull off his sweater, I lean up and kiss each of his chiseled abs, dragging my tongue between them until I feel him tremble beneath my lips. I grab his shoulders and flip us around until I'm straddling his lap. I can feel him hard and thick beneath the fabric of his jeans, and there's nothing more that I want right now than to taste

Maren Moore

him, to wrap my lips around his cock and bring him to his knees.

He watches from below me as I unbutton his jeans, slowly dragging the zipper down. His cock is already straining against the thin fabric of his boxer briefs. I palm the length, squeezing him in my hand until he hisses.

"Suck my cock, baby. Show me how much you deserve to be on the naughty list." His voice is rough and husky as he works the waistband of his briefs down to free his cock. He quickly sheds his jeans along with the briefs, leaving him completely naked beneath me. A bead of precum leaks from the tip of his hard cock, and I want to lick it off. When I lean forward to swipe my tongue along the slit, he stops me.

"Wanna look at those pretty tits as you choke on my cock, Snowflake."

His fingers wrestle with the clasp of my bra, unhooking it and pulling it down so my chest is on full display for him. He cups each one in his hand, tweaking the nipple roughly. "So pretty. Almost as pretty as your pink little pussy."

I fist his cock tightly, pumping it from base to tip as my tongue darts out again and laps at the salty precum seeping from his slit.

He moans, his hands leaving my tits to fly to my hair just as I close my mouth around the head of his cock, sucking hard in tandem with my fist that's circling his base.

"Fuuuuuuuck."

The groan that tumbles from his lips has my hips grinding, trying to stifle the throb in my pussy.

Palming my head, he thrusts his hips up slightly, causing his cock to slide even deeper into my mouth and down my throat. I gag slightly, then exhale through my nose, pushing

158

to take him even further until I can feel the head of his cock rutting against the back of my throat.

"I want to fuck your throat, Snowflake. If it's too much, tap and I'll stop."

I nod around his length, pulling my hands free as his fingers tangle in my hair and cradle my head, guiding me down his length until he's so deep in my throat that my eyes are watering when he begins to thrust.

"That's it. Open up for me like a good girl. You can take all of it—take it all for me."

I want to please him, I want to drive him as crazy with desire as he drives me, so I suck in air through my nose and do as I'm told, opening my throat and going down the rest of the way. His thrusts are short and choppy as he fucks my face, gripping my hair with fervor but not causing me any pain.

"Fuck, Emma. You take my cock so well. Like the most perfect fucking girl."

His praise only spurs me on, and I reach between us and palm his balls, rolling them between my fingers. I can feel them tightening, ready to fill my throat with his cum, but he stops abruptly, pulling free of my mouth.

It shouldn't be so hot to see the string of my spit connecting us or the fact that he's glistening with it from being so deep in my throat, but it is.

It's insanely hot, and it only makes me want him more. Makes my pussy more wet for him.

"I want my cum inside you" is all he says, flipping us over until my back hits the bed and he's hovering between my parted thighs. He makes quick work of my jeans and panties, tugging them off my body in a single movement that leaves me bare and spread out beneath him.

"I'll never get tired of seeing your pussy seeping for me. Seeing the mess you make. All this just from taking my cock down your throat."

Using his fingers, he spreads me open wide and then spits, watching as it trails down my clit to my entrance. He latches onto my clit, sucking it into his mouth roughly, rolling it between his lips, varying pressure as my spine arches from the bed with pleasure. I can't help but tangle my fingers into his hair, desperately holding on as he eats me like a man possessed.

He takes his time, lapping at every inch of me, his tongue circling my entrance over and over again before finally thrusting inside me as he thumbs my clit, my arousal dripping from me.

It only takes minutes for my legs to shake and my hips to buck against his mouth as my body teeters on the edge of orgasm.

But before he lets me come, he pulls back and moves over me until he's at eye level, fitting his hips between my open thighs.

"I can't wait another second to be inside you," he pants, reaching between us and dragging the head of his cock through my wetness, nudging my clit with a small snap of his hips. "Need to feel you come on my cock."

Nodding, I hitch my leg higher on his hip just as he slides in a single inch, both of us moaning at the sensation. Even after the foreplay, he's so big that it takes a second for my body to adjust to his size, drenched or not.

His fingers lace in mine, and he lifts my hands above my

head as his hips punch forward, thrusting until he's buried to the hilt.

"Jackson," I breathe.

My head feels light, my chest tight with the fullness of him inside me, and I desperately want him to move, to push me over the edge.

"Move, please," I beg, tightening my fingers in his. I'm not above pleading if it means tumbling off the precipice he's edged me on.

Thankfully, he obliges, withdrawing slowly and then surging forward, hitting the perfect spot inside of me that has my toes curling, incoherent words leaving my lips.

"I'm not going to last, Emma. I need you with me," he pants, picking up his rhythm. His hips slap against mine as he fucks me, rough and uncontrolled. The erotic sounds of our joint arousal fill the room.

Dropping one of his hands to my clit, he circles it roughly, alternating pressure until I can feel the orgasm building and building and building. I grip his ass, pulling him into me as he rocks his hips, arousal spiraling inside of me until it's pulsing. I can feel it prickling beneath the surface, ready to detonate.

Jackson kisses me hungrily, deepening it as his thrusts turn erratic and wild.

"Melt for me, Snowflake," he rasps.

Pleasure rocks through me as my orgasm invades me, body and mind, sending me barreling toward euphoria like I've never known. My body tenses, and my belly quivers from the intensity.

I hear him groan, low and rough, before he thrusts deep

one final time and comes, hot ropes of cum spurting inside of me, filling me, claiming me.

There's no doubt in my mind, after this moment, that I'm wholly, completely Jackson Pearce's.

A few moments later, he drops to the bed, rolling onto his side, still buried inside of me, gathering me against his chest. Our skin is covered in a sheen of sweat, our chests heaving as we try to catch our breath. Skin to skin, I feel more complete, more whole than I ever have.

In his arms, I feel safe.

"I'm crazy about you. You realize that, don't you?" he mumbles against my hair, tightening his arms around me.

I can feel him seeping out of me from where we're still connected, wetting both of us. It's obscene, dirty, but yet, it makes me feel... *his.*

"I'm pretty crazy about you too."

His chest vibrates as he chuckles. "You just blew my fucking mind, Snowflake. That was so dirty and so damn hot."

"I think you bring out this side of me. It's never... been like that with anyone else," I tell him honestly. I don't think I've ever felt this way about anyone, the way that I feel about Jackson. And it's not just in the bedroom.

"For me either."

For a moment, neither of us speaks, the room quiet, only the sound of our labored breathing filling the room until he tenderly pulls out of me and leaves me on the bed as he walks to the bathroom.

I don't think I could move right now, even if I wanted to. My limbs feel impossibly heavy, almost as tired as my eyes, and I curl into the plush comforter as sleep begins to creep its way in.

The bed dips, and then Jackson's there, fingers pressing into my thighs as he parts them, using a warm rag to clean me.

"That was sweet," I murmur, my eyes still closed, a soft smile on my lips.

He chuckles. "I told you I would take care of you, Snowflake. I meant it."

I hum and wait for him to crawl back into the bed, sighing when he does and hauls me against his warm body. His lips press against my neck, and I burrow into his hold.

I'm sleepy. And sated. And *deliriously...* happy.

"Sleep, Emma. Tomorrow's a busy day, and you need rest."

It's the last day before the party, which means final touches and praying that everything goes smoothly.

Sometimes it feels like the entire town might be against us, especially when it comes to this party, but then there are moments like this, and it just feels... *right.* And all the rest fades away.

17 /
emma

Making the list... checking it twice.

My head is pounding so loudly that I can practically hear the thrum in my ears, and it shows no signs of stopping. I scan the list once more, double-checking each item that I've marked off.

- Dress - check
- Favor bags - check
- Ask Jackson to double-check place settings (unconfirmed)
- Electronic equipment for music - Jackson currently picking up
- Also ask Jackson to make sure the band has everything they need to set up
- Caterer: confirmed setting up - check
- Cake: delivered - check

Officially, eight hours till party time, and things are going *surprisingly* smoothly… aside from the massive migraine that I've had since this morning that I'm sure is stress related.

If I'm honest, all I want to do is crawl back into Jackson's ridiculously comfy bed and sleep for the next twelve hours. My body is sore in all of the best places from last night, and as anxious as I am for this party to go off without a hitch, I'm looking forward to catching up on sleep without the stress of this party hanging over my head.

"Emma, darling?"

The voice pulls me from my thoughts, and I glance up to see my mother walking toward me. She's wearing a two-piece suit, heels, and a matching pair of pearls, flawless as always.

"Hi, Mom," I say, stepping in to give her a hug, to-do list still clutched in my hand. "You know the party doesn't start for another eight hours, right?"

She nods. "Of course. I just wanted to check in on you. It's been a couple weeks since you stopped by the house, but I know how hard you've been working on the party. Is there anything I can do to help?"

Stealing a glance at my list, I shake my head. "Nope. I think we've got it covered. I just need to get home and change, then get back up here so I can make sure everything is delivered and set up correctly."

Mom looks around the building, her eyes raking over the decorations, the table settings, the lights twinkling along the rafters courtesy of Jackson and his brothers.

"Everything truly looks amazing, darling. I'm so proud of you," she says, reaching out to pat my arm affectionately. "I see you've kept the Worthington place card holders—they are a lovely addition. Oh! And the tree. Beautiful. Your father and I are not overjoyed about having to be with the Pearce family tonight, but we will be here for you. He needs to see all of the hard work you've put in despite the adversity you've faced having to work with... them."

"Well, thank you for the compliment and for being here tonight," I say, suddenly overcome with the urge to hug my mom. I toss my arms around her and hold her close against me. This year might be different when it comes to our family tradition, and I know she's not happy that it's changing, but it means a lot to me that she's here.

I feel her pat my back and whisper against my ear, "I'd do anything for you, darling girl."

I didn't realize how much I needed this until now. The last few weeks have been a whirlwind of different emotions, and in the midst of all of it, I feel different.

Happier. Lighter.

"I love you, Mom."

"I love you too, darling," she says, and I swear that I hear her sniffle, but she clears her throat and pulls back. "Goodness, enough of that. I'll let you get back to it, and I'll see you tonight, okay? Oh, and you may want to turn the heat up in here—it's quite chilly. You'll want to make sure all of our guests are nice and warm."

"I've been so busy setting up I didn't even notice. I'll let them know to turn it up. See you tonight." With a smile and a wave goodbye, she walks out of the door, leaving me alone.

I feel better, less nervous, after talking to Mom, and now I'm ready to get home, put on the most beautiful dress I've ever owned, and throw the best dang party that Strawberry Hollow has ever had. All with Jackson by my side.

After one last run-through, I leave the catering company to finish setting up, let the maintenance guys know to turn up the heat, then grab my bag and head out the door.

THE MOMENT I walk back across the threshold, I know something is very, very wrong.

It's freezing.

It's barely three o'clock in the afternoon, and I can see my breath… inside Town Hall.

Of course, I'm already completely dressed for tonight in my party dress and favorite Louboutins. I wanted to make sure I was ready and back here in case there were any last-minute issues, which clearly… there are.

"Has anyone seen Jackson?" I ask Gary, the maintenance and lawn guy for the city, as he passes by, a look of worry on his face.

Great, even Gary looks worried. Something is definitely wrong.

He doesn't say anything but points toward the back room, where moments later, Jackson comes strolling out. I expected him to be dressed for the party, but instead, he's got his signature worn jeans and a flannel on, and he's covered in black dirt with a large wrench in his hand.

Oh God.

He looks *irrationally* hot right now, but I can't even focus on that because I am now full-blown panicking.

"*Please* tell me that it's just me and it isn't actually this cold in here," I tell him when he stops in front of me.

I can tell just by the expression on his face that that isn't the case at all.

"I wish I could, Snowflake," he says softly, gently, as if I'm a wounded animal about to flee. "Heating's out. The furnace should've been replaced a damn decade ago. I tried but couldn't fix it."

Groaning, I drop my face to my hands, tears welling in my eyes. I knew things were going too smoothly. There was no possible way everything was going to go that great.

I was waiting for the other shoe to drop, and it did.

"Hey," Jackson says as he sets the wrench down onto a nearby chair, tipping my chin up to look at him. "We'll figure it out, Emma. It's going to be okay."

"Jackson, it is *not* going to be okay!" I sniffle as his thumb swipes along my cheek, brushing away the stray tear that has fallen. "God, I had this perfect plan. Every single detail planned out and even a plan B, although I was sure that I would never need it. Well, guess what I didn't plan for? The venue not being usable. This is a disaster, and now the entire party is going to be ruined. We put so much hard work into making this place go from drab and dreary to a winter wonderland, and it's ruined."

I'm full-on crying now, and I know my makeup is probably smeared down my face at this point, but I'm so upset and disappointed.

"Fuck, I hate seeing you cry, Emma," Jackson says. "Baby, I will fix this. Maybe not the furnace, but this party is far from ruined. We're going to have the best damn party that Strawberry Hollow has ever seen."

I want to laugh at how confident his words sound, but I'm too distraught at this point.

"What can we do? It's not like we have a ton of spare buildings ready to host the entire town, Jackson. And the food? The decorations? The band?" My chest starts to feel tight when I start to think of all the moving pieces that I need to align for this damn party to happen.

His chest rises as he exhales, still holding me to him, and then he pulls back to look at me. "I've got an idea. You might hate it, but I think it's the best one we've got, Snowflake."

At this point, we're going to have to take what we can get, or this party is not going to happen. And to save both of our reputations and records, there *has* to be a party.

"I'm listening."

He nods, a serious expression on his handsome face. "We have the party at the barn on my parents' property."

"Jackson..." I say, my eyes wide as I start to shake my head.

"Just hear me out. It's big enough for everyone, and we've got an extra-large hearth in there with plenty of firewood. We've got lights and electricity running to it already, so all we'd have to do is get everything moved over and then have Wayne and Mayor Davis spread the word that the location has changed. It'll solve the problem."

Pulling my lip between my teeth, I mull it over. I mean, it *could* work. But I think my parents are going to be extremely unhappy about it being on Pearce land, in the barn where they always host their annual party, instead of somewhere neutral like Town Hall.

It's already enough that we're getting our entire families together under one roof. But if we do this... it'll be a *Pearce* roof. Hell, they might not even come at that point.

But what other option is there? The barn has everything we need to pull this off if we work quickly. We have absolutely no time to waste.

"Okay. Let's do it," I exhale, trying to rein in my rampant

emotions. Logically, I know this is the best plan for everyone. "But how are we going to get everything over to the barn on such short notice? I mean... we have so much to do and so little time, Jackson. It's seriously going to take some kind of Christmas miracle for us to actually be able to make this happen. My perfectly curated plan has fallen apart."

This time, he chuckles, and I love the way his lip tugs up into a grin, momentarily taking my mind off the fact the entire party is falling apart around us. I wish we could just sneak away back to his house with Marley and Mo, and I could watch them running in the yard in their new sweaters. I decided next I'm going to knit them some adorable little booties for their paws so they don't get cold when they're running in the snow.

"Well, that's why you've got me. We're moving on to plan... C."

"Was there a plan C until right now?"

"Nope." He grins. "But if there's anything I've learned since meeting you, it's that we absolutely need a plan. Especially when it comes to things like this. So now... we're going with plan C, and it'll be *amazing*. I'm going to go make some calls, get my crew up here with the work trucks, get this loaded up, and move locations. I need to give my parents a heads-up too."

I nod. "Okay, and I'll talk with the caterer and the band and... call my parents, as well as Wayne and Mayor Davis. They can let all the residents know we're moving, and then I'll start packing up all of the decorations and table settings."

Toeing off my red-soled heels, I lose four inches as my bare feet hit the floor, but I've got a thousand things to do and not enough time.

This calls for the big guns.

"Let's do this, Snowflake."

"IS SHE ALWAYS LIKE THIS?" Jensen grumbles as he moves the twelve-foot tree a few inches to the left for the... fourth time.

While the Pearce barn has a certain rustic charm to it, I'm still working with *far* less space than Town Hall, and with the last-minute venue change, I have to put in double the work to make sure this party is everything it should be and more.

Jackson laughs. "Yep."

"I'm sorry!" I mutter, an apologetic expression on my face. "I think it's just kind of leaning to the right a little, and the tree is such an important part of the party. It really sets the tone... and my parents will have a fit if it's not here."

Jackson's brother grumbles but moves the tree to the left again, and finally, it sits straight in the perfect position. I hurry over with the box of ornaments and ribbon and start to redecorate it.

Thankfully, a few of Jackson's siblings and a few of his crew members came to help us put everything back up. If we didn't have them, there is no possible way we could've gotten this done. We have T-minus two hours to make sure everything is done before guests arrive.

"How did Jed take it when you told him about the last-minute change?" Jackson asks as he climbs the ladder to hang another snowflake garland.

"Well, there weren't any other options. He should've

replaced the furnace years ago when it needed to be replaced, and we wouldn't be in this predicament right now. So, he said he would take care of it, and that was that. I think he sent out a text blast, and Wayne is doing house calls for the people who aren't into technology."

"Good. Josie said she spread the word to all the teachers at her school, so that probably helped. And… your parents?"

"Uh, they took it as expected. I love my parents with all of my heart, and yes, their approval means a lot to me. It always has. I respect their opinion, but if they decide not to come tonight simply because it's *here*, then that would be their loss. I would be hurt because this party is such a special tradition for us, but I also can't force them to be here when they don't want to be," I say, feeling a twinge of disappointment at the thought of my parents not showing up tonight.

Climbing down from the ladder, he takes the ornament I'm holding from my hand and places it on the tree, then pulls me into his arms and kisses me gently. For a second, I forget where we are and who is around us, until I pull back, my eyes wide.

"Jackson…"

"Fuck it. Let them look. You're mine, Emma, and I want the entire damn world to know it. I'm not hiding the way I feel about you, and if anyone has anything to say about it, then they know exactly where to find me," he says, a fierce look in his eyes.

My heart feels like it's in my throat as he speaks. Out of all of the scenarios that I expected to happen when it came to this joint party, falling for Jackson Pearce was *not* one of them.

And I *know* that I'm falling for him.

By the way my heart thrashes in my chest every time he

smiles. How he acts grumpy when it comes to Mo and Marley but melts like butter anytime they're around. With how tender and gentle he can be with me but also doesn't hesitate to call me on the things I'm wrong about.

I'm falling for him, and it's a scary thought. Not just because of our family's stupid history but because it feels like I am completely and totally out of control of my feelings.

Being in control, being able to compartmentalize things, it's how I protect myself, and right now, I feel like I'm bared open wide for him with nothing to protect the most vulnerable part of me: my heart.

"Are you sure?" I say, swallowing the thick ball of emotion at the base of my throat as his arms tighten around me.

"Never been more sure of anything, Emma. What I feel for you is not temporary, and it sure as fuck is not something I'm going to hide." Leaning down, he brushes his nose against mine as he plants a gentle kiss at the corner of my lip. "Once all of this is over, we can have a bigger conversation about all this, but I need you to know that I'm all in, and I'm not going anywhere."

He kisses me again, his hand cradling my jaw, so tenderly I could melt into a puddle right on the floor.

"Okay," I say, nodding. "Tonight we can talk, after the party."

Jackson nods and steps back, immediately causing me to miss his touch. But if he doesn't put distance between us, then we're never going to finish getting the barn party-ready.

"Tell me where you need me," he says.

I direct him to the few things that need to be hung, and then I busy myself covering the tables that we brought over from Town Hall, resetting them with the elegant centerpieces, place cards, and silverware.

With the help of his crew and the catering company and with some patience from the band, we manage to get everything set back up with twenty minutes to spare.

And... it doesn't look half-bad.

It actually looks quite charming, much cozier than the outdated Town Hall ever did. The fireplace is crackling, the band set up nearby, leaving a decent-sized dance floor. The Worthington tree twinkles, the flocked branches full of ornaments, ribbon, and lights. It's exactly what this space needed to tie it together. Glittering snowflakes and faux snow are strewn around the rafters, draped from one side to the other, along with twinkling fairy lights that set the tone. It looks classy but also welcoming and cozy. The barn turned out to be the perfect setting for a party that is somehow *both* Worthington and Pearce.

The six-tier *gingerbread* cake is covered in white icing, with piped snowflakes around the base, and sugared ice is sprinkled from top to bottom. It's beautiful, and judging by the way it smells, it's going to be as delicious as Jackson promised it would be. I guess not going with vanilla was the right choice. Something I'm sure Jackson will love to tease me about.

I'm beyond proud of the work we've done and even prouder that despite everything going wrong at the last minute, we somehow made it way better than what it originally would've been.

"Looks good, Emma," Jude affirms, placing the last of the tea light candles into their holders on the tables.

I smile. "Well, I definitely couldn't have done it without your brother or any of your help."

"Yeah, would you look at that... a Pearce and a Worthington, working together. Who would've ever thought?" He chuckles. "I'm glad we could help though. It was kind of nice helping today. Makes me think next year maybe *I* should be in charge of the party."

"Not a chance in hell, baby brother. Sorry, but my girl is the *only* one for the job," Jackson interjects as he walks up, lacing his fingers in mine. "Ready to do this?"

"Yes. Let's show this town what happens when two *'feuding families'* come together and throw the party of a century."

18 /
jackson

A Very Festive Feud

I'm standing in the middle of a crowded room, the entire town surrounding me, and the only thing I see is Emma Worthington.

If you had told me a month ago that I would be falling in love with the girl I've spent the majority of my life hating, I would've laughed in your face and told you that you'd lost your mind.

Yet, here I stand, hopelessly in love with her.

I watch as she tips her head back, laughter pouring from her lips, her blonde curls swaying at her waist in response to whatever Quinn Grant said. I've been watching her for the last ten minutes, silently sipping my beer.

She's so fucking beautiful and completely in her element right now.

Despite her worries and all the obstacles, the party is a hit. I mean, as much as it can be with our families on separate sides of the room, pretending like the other doesn't exist, both using the residents of Strawberry Hollow as a buffer between them.

It's clear that people are enjoying themselves, the band keeping the room lively, but there's still… unresolved tension hanging heavily in the air.

Everyone is kind of standing around, waiting with bated breath for the other shoe to drop, and I don't blame them.

"Man, a lot happened in three weeks."

Glancing up, I see Oliver walking up with a grin as he follows my gaze to Emma.

Isn't that the truth.

But I shrug. "What do you mean?"

"Don't act like you're not completely wrapped around that girl's finger, Pearce." Laughing, he tips his beer back. "You haven't taken your eyes off of her since she walked through the door."

"Yeah, well, she's kind of had me wrapped around her finger since day one. I'm pretty sure fighting over a nutcracker with her and getting tossed in the drunk tank for a night may have been the best thing that has ever happened to me. I never stood a chance."

He chuckles. "I knew the day you sat in my bar that you were a goner. Hell, you didn't even know it then."

The band switches to "I'll Be Home For Christmas," and that's my cue.

"Sorry, man, gotta go dance with my girl."

"Go, go. Stop by the bar next week so we can catch up now that you're off party-planning duty."

With a nod, I leave him and make my way across the barn to Emma and Quinn. I slide my hand around her hip, and she jumps in surprise.

"Hi." I grin. "Sorry to interrupt, Quinn. Can I steal Emma away for a dance?"

Quinn's eyebrow rises, and she nods, clearly shocked that the two of us aren't at each other's throats.

I told Emma I was done hiding, and I meant it. The means here, at our party, I want to dance with her and drown out the damn world.

Turning to her, I ask, "Can I have this dance?" and offer her my hand.

She slides her palm into mine, and I whisk her away to the edge of the dance floor, choosing a less crowded spot in the back so we can talk. Her hands clasp behind my neck as we slowly sway to the music, my arms tight around her waist, pressing her against me. Thankfully, her parents are on the far side of the barn, so we're hidden from their view by the crowd. They've been at a table in the corner all night, not trying to hide their distaste for being here.

"You know, I never got to tell you how beautiful you look tonight," I murmur.

She grins cheekily. "Oh! That's right, you didn't. But I mean, if you want to tell me now... I'm listening."

"That *mouth*." I lean forward, nipping at her lips as she squeals quietly against my mouth. When I pull back, her cheeks are flushed red from laughing, those painted red lips parted. "I can't stop looking at you, Snowflake. That dress, hugging all of your curves... the red on your lips, the happiness in your eyes. But even without anything else, just *you*... you're the most beautiful girl in this room, without question."

"Are you... trying to get in my pants, Jackson Pearce?" she responds, and I can't help the laugh that falls from my lips.

This. Girl.

"That depends. How am I doing?"

Her hands tighten in the hair at my nape, and she rises on her toes, pulling me down to her lips. Just before they brush mine, she whispers, "I'd say your chances are looking preeeetttttty good."

"Um... sorry to interrupt."

We both pull back to see Mark from the hardware store standing there with red cheeks, looking extremely embarrassed to have interrupted the two of us.

"Mark? Is everything okay?" Emma says as she takes a step back.

Mark scratches his head and scrunches his nose. "Well, I mean, I guess that depends on who you ask, really? Uh... there might be a bit of a disagreement happening over by the bar area."

Emma freezes, her eyes going wide as panic floods her face. "*Shit,*" she curses, then brushes past Mark.

I follow after her, throwing a *sorry* over my shoulder.

The scene is apparently only beginning to unfold as we both stop in front of the bar. Jensen and Dad are having words with Mr. and Mrs. Worthington, and I can feel the tension escalating heavily in the air.

Fuck. I was hoping this wouldn't happen.

"Yeah, well, it seems like you got exactly what you wanted, then, doesn't it?" Emma's dad snorts, turning his nose up even higher if that were at all possible, and I do not foresee this ending well.

Jensen shakes his head before retorting, "Right, like we had something to do with the twenty-five-year-old furnace going out. That thing hasn't been used in years, and trust me, I'm pretty sure I can speak for everyone in my family when I say that *we* want you here about as much as *you* want to be here."

Emma stiffens as we move our gaze from one side of the argument to the other.

Her dad's face is turning redder by the second, and even Mrs. Worthington trying to placate him is not helping. "Wouldn't surprise me if you sabotaged it, just like your family has for years! Don't act like this is the first time one of you has done something just to spite our family."

"And *your* hands are clean?" my dad adds, questioning in his tone. I think he's trying not to fuel this argument, but his words are terse and his lips flatten into a line as he bites his tongue.

"Cleaner than *yours*," Mr. Worthington says. "I mean, if it wasn't for *your* son, then my daughter wouldn't be forced to put this entire thing together or end up in jail or with a damn criminal record!"

The band has completely stopped playing, and the entire room has gone eerily quiet. Not only are our families having a fight in the middle of a party Emma and I have worked our asses off to make happen, but the entire town has a front-row seat to our drama. *Again.*

"Daddy!" Emma cries.

Her father holds his hand up, silencing her as he drags his gaze back to Jensen and Dad. Now, Jude, Josie, and Jameson have joined, standing behind them.

I'm not even going to insert myself into this conversation. If he wants to believe that I'm the sole reason that this shit happened, then that's on him. Arguing with him in front of the entire town is not going to change that, and I'm not going to hurt Emma that way.

"This has been going on for years. Your family is always trying to sabotage us, to spite us, to do whatever you can to make sure that our party isn't successful," Mr. Worthington says. "Not only did you steal our party tradition, but over the years, you've stolen Christmas lights from our yard, flipped our decorations upside down, filled our mailbox with coal, toilet papered our outdoor fir trees the night before our party. You should be ashamed of yourselves for your *unruly* behavior."

Ma walks over, standing in front of my dad with her chin raised high and a finger that's pointed directly at Mr. Worthington's face. "Now, that is *enough*. You are just as guilty in this silly feud as we are. I think we can all admit that we have done things that we shouldn't have, things that we are not proud of… but you cannot live in glass houses, Mr. Worthington. Placing blame on us means accepting the very same blame for yourself. If anyone should be ashamed, it's *you* for creating this entire spectacle that is neither the time nor the place!"

"How about you keep your little… *ugly* sweaters and your disgusting gingerbread cake, and we can leave. As simple as that. We want no part in this farce of a party," Mrs. Worthington says. "It's clearly all about *your* family getting what *you* wanted, and we were never welcome in the first place."

I see Emma's frustration, her sadness, her disappointment start to boil over. Her fists clenched at her side, she storms forward and steps between our families.

"*Enough!*" she says so loudly that it echoes off the wooden walls of the barn. "God, look at all of you. Fighting in the middle of a damn Christmas party over who has done what.

You're pointing fingers, saying things that are hurtful and absolutely not true. This has gone on long enough, and it ends. Right here. *Right now.*"

"Emma, with all due respect, I don't think you have any right to speak to my family right now," Jameson says with a sneer.

Nope. *Fuck no.*

I walk directly over to Emma, facing my family and my brother who's clearly lost his goddamn mind speaking to her that way, and I grab her hand, lacing her fingers in mine, showing a united front.

"Brother, with all due respect, the next time you disrespect her that way, we're going to have our own problem that we'll have to resolve outside."

Josie's jaw drops in shock, but she recovers quickly, plastering on a grin, then giving me a sneaky thumbs-up.

"Look, Emma is right. This stupid godforsaken *'feud'* has gone on for years, and it's honestly fucking exhausting. Give it up. Do you even remember what started this? Why are we even fighting? Why has this gone on for as long as it has? Genuinely, can you even tell me that?" I look back and forth between my family and hers.

Her father works his jaw, then rolls his eyes. "Of course I do. Your family decided after moving to town that you were too good for our annual party. The Worthingtons have been hosting the town for Christmas practically since the town was founded—it's a respected institution. Yet when the Pearces came to town, you never bothered to respond to the invitation. Oh, but even better! You decided the following year that you'd throw your *own* party. On the same day. And didn't bother to invite our family. You tried to steal our family's legacy!"

"What?" Ma says, her brow furrowing. "You invited our family to your party?"

"Of course we did! We invited everyone in town and have since the very first party," Mrs. Worthington adds. "It's something our family takes pride in, and we were excited to have someone new in Strawberry Hollow. Someone new we could bring into the town tradition that we Worthingtons hold so dear. You snubbed our party, not even dignifying us with a response. We don't expect every single person invited to come... but then you never even bothered to say hello or speak to us around town. And then you *willfully* scheduled your party the next year on top of ours, a century-old Strawberry Hollow tradition? It felt... well, it felt like a slap directly in the face."

Emma and I whip our heads back to Ma, who's wearing an expression of total bewilderment. She runs her hand over her mouth and shakes her head. "Amelia, we never *got* an invitation to the Worthington party when we first moved here, have never gotten an invitation to one of your parties *ever*. We thought that you were excluding us that year because we were outsiders and not a true part of Strawberry Hollow. That's why we never bothered to say anything when we saw you in town because we thought it was done purposefully, that we were being purposefully excluded since everyone else was invited. You really did invite us?"

Holy fuck. Are they saying...

"Yes, of course we did. Why would we purposely exclude you? We only snubbed *you* because we thought you were snubbing *us*," Mr. Worthington says as Mrs. Worthington nods, adding, "We felt as if we were simply reciprocating your behavior."

My dad shakes his head. "Assumptions were made, on both parts. It seems like we all acted in a way that does not accurately represent our character. Who we are as people. Who we are as a family. We've forgotten how Christmas *should* be celebrated. I'll admit we did have our own party, but it was only because we figured we wouldn't be invited to any parties going forward. All we wanted to do was make new friends and truly make Strawberry Hollow our home. We didn't know. And being so caught up in all of it, we also turned a blind eye to the boys' antics, and it has just all gotten out of hand. I'm sorry for that."

"This was all a very *monumental*... miscommunication," Emma whispers, disbelief lacing her tone.

Josie groans. "Ugh, I *hate* the miscommunication trope." She mutters the words under her breath but loud enough for me to hear. That girl and her books.

"Oh dear... it does seem to be that way." Ma nods, her shoulders scrunching up in embarrassment.

For the first time in history, our families seem to be *agreeing* on something. That something being the fact that for the last three decades, we've been fighting over... *nothing*.

"You're telling me that our families have been feuding for all of this time over a *fucking misplaced invitation*?" I say.

Guilt marks my parents' features, and when I look at the Worthingtons, they're sporting a similar expression.

"I'm... I'm sorry, Lucy. To you, to your whole family, for all of it. This was so silly and juvenile, and I can't believe I partook in something like this blindly for years. That I never tried to resolve things sooner," Emma says with sincerity.

"Emma, it wasn't just you. It was *all* of us, sweetheart," Ma tells her. She pulls Emma into a warm hug before she walks over to Mrs. Worthington. "I'm so very sorry that this happened, Amelia. That's not enough, simply saying that I'm sorry, but I think it's the only place to start."

Mrs. Worthington nods, her face softening. "I'm sorry as well, Lucy. Deeply. For everything over the years, and for you believing for so long that we didn't want you at our party. That couldn't have been further from the truth. But, we did try on... occasion to interfere with your parties over the years, trying to shut them down so everyone would come to ours, and that was so wrong of us to do. Spiteful, and I'm just *so* sorry for everything." She sniffles, overcome with emotion. "Goodness, we have really mucked this party up, haven't we? It's Christmas. Do you think... we could maybe put this behind us? I know there are a lot of bridges to rebuild, but I think I can speak for my family." She glances at her husband, who nods. "We'd really like to try to start over. For the sake of all of us."

"There is nothing I would love more," Ma says, shocking the shit out of me and reaching for Mrs. Worthington and dragging her in for a big hug. "And I think we should make each other a promise, family to family, that if there is ever something that happens like this again, we go directly to the source and never let something cause such a divide again."

"I think that is perfect. And I'm also sorry for what I said about your cake flavor... It's actually *delicious*, and... I think your sweater is absolutely darling," Mrs. Worthington replies as she pulls back.

Ma laughs, the sound ringing out around us. "You know, I

think I have an extra inside that would fit you. Let's go grab it?"

Mrs. Worthington nods, and when she walks off with Ma, I see my dad approaching Mr. Worthington with his hand extended.

Seeing them shake hands after everything that has happened makes me feel grateful. Then I realize that the rest of the party has picked back up like it never stopped, only this time, the air in the room is inherently... *lighter.* The thick tension is gone. The band is playing low in the background again, people are laughing, and the smell of gingerbread combined with the crackling hearth fills the air. The big invisible line down the middle of the room has suddenly vanished, and it feels like for the first time tonight, people are genuinely having fun.

Emma spoke about a Christmas miracle earlier, and it seems like we got one after all.

Her hand tightens in mine, and when I glance at her, I see fresh tears of happiness on her cheeks.

"Did that actually just happen?" She laughs, brushing them away. We're in the middle of the party, completely surrounded by people, but I can't wait another damn second to hold her.

I pull her to me until she's tight in my arms and I'm staring at the deep blue of her irises. "I think it did, Snowflake. You know, since everyone's sharing their feelings, I think now might be as good of a time as any to have that talk."

Her brow arches. "Oh?"

"I'm crazy about you, Emma Worthington. Head over

heels, Snowflake, and loving you is easily the best decision I've ever made."

"You love me?" Her breath hitches.

Grasping her chin in my fingers, I lean closer. "I do. *Almost* as much as you love sticky notes and to-do lists."

When she laughs, a dopey smile forms on my lips as she says, "I love you too, Jackson Pearce. Even *with* your aversion to organization and despite the fact that you are, in fact, terrible at building gingerbread houses."

"There's always next year, and now that I've got you as my partner, I'm not giving you up." Brushing my lips across hers, I whisper, "Here's to new *and* old traditions… together."

"Together has *never* sounded better."

And to think… this all started with a very *festive* feud.

THE END

epilogue

Emma

9 months later

"What are you working on?" Jackson says behind me, startling me as I sit at his kitchen table, my head bent over my notebook as I scribble notes on the paper.

I jump, my hand clutching my chest. "*Jesus*, Jackson, you scared the hell out of me!"

"Well, I *did* call your name a few times, Snowflake. You were in the zone." He chuckles, pressing his lips to my temple as he slides his arms around me, holding me to him.

Even after all of this time together, nine months of blissful happiness, I still can't believe that he's *mine*. That somehow, our love was a result of that stupid feud that controlled our families for so long. That we were lucky enough to have each other in the end.

"Sorry, I was focusing."

"I see that. A new design?"

I shake my head. "No, actually, I'm getting a head start on the... party for this year."

189

Jackson laughs. "Of course, you are. You know we've got three months till Christmas, right?"

"Of course, I know that," I say, my fingers running along the beard on his cheeks. I love when he grows it out some, and I love it even more when my thighs are scratched raw from it. "But as you know, having a plan is important, and I don't want to wait till the last minute. *Ever* again. It's chaotic and stressful."

"You're right. Well, you know if you need me, I'm here. Although, I think this is definitely a you, your mom, Ma, and Josie kind of thing now."

He's right, and I can't even begin to explain how happy it makes me to say that. Not only did I get Jackson out of this feud, but I got his family, who is wonderful, supportive, and kind. They are just as important and special to me as he is, so being able to work with both my mom and his mom and sister this year on my favorite Christmas tradition?

Indescribable.

Hence getting an early start in… September. I just can't help it. I'm feeling the Christmas spirit already.

"Yep, we've already decided to meet for dinner at your parents' house this weekend while you and the guys are doing… *men* things."

And by men things, I mean both of our dads and his brothers all taking a trip to go to his family's cabin in the mountains. That leaves me at home with the girls, the best wine, and all of the Christmas planning.

The perfect place to be.

"Sounds like you've got it all figured out, then. Gotta show you something though. Come see," he says as he lets me go and nods toward the living room.

I set my pen down on the table and hop out the chair, following behind him through the hallway to the spare bedroom at the end. My brow furrows in confusion, and he chuckles, swinging the door open.

"I've been doing some reorganizing, and I made room for your obscene amount of Christmas decorations. Don't think they're all gonna fit in my attic."

Well, I mean, they fit in my attic just fine... *wait.*

"Why would I bring my Christmas decorations to your house, Jackson?"

He shrugs. "'Cause don't you think it's about time you *officially* moved in? You've got more stuff here than at your house at this point anyway. Plus... it would make Mo and Marley happy."

Hearing their names, they come padding down the hallway with wide puppy eyes that make my heart squeeze.

I love these babies just as much as I love their daddy.

"I think... maybe that can be arranged," I say, moving my hands over his chest before clasping them behind his neck. "I don't know though. Are you sure you have enough room? You *might* have to sleep outside if I have to choose between storing the Christmas decorations or you."

"Go check out the closet," he says, nodding toward the door opposite us. "Let me know if you think there's enough room."

I walk across the empty spare room and open the closet door, my jaw falling open in shock as my hand flies to my mouth.

Inside is a nutcracker. But not just any nutcracker.

The very same nutcracker from the general store last year.

When I turn back toward him, he's right there, his hands sliding around my waist and hauling me to him.

"You've had it all this time?" I say in disbelief.

He nods, a grin on his lips. "Of course, I did. Felt like now was the perfect time to give it to you. After all, it's the reason why we fell in love in the first place. Full circle, Snowflake. Move in with me and put up as many damn decorations as you want. This place needs all the love you have to give it."

Rising on my tiptoes, I kiss him, slipping my tongue past his lips and into his mouth while he holds me tightly against his hard body.

With him, I feel safe. I feel loved. I feel protected. I feel cherished.

There's nothing I want more than to make me living here a permanent thing.

"I guess I could move in. On *one* condition…" I whisper, my hands behind his neck, holding him to me.

"And what's that?"

"You let me put the decorations up… now."

His deep groan turns into a laugh, and he shakes his head. "I don't care if you want to leave the damn things up all year round. I just need you in my bed, permanently."

Grinning, I pull back and untangle myself from his arms, dragging my hand down his chest to his stomach before pulling it away abruptly. "Well… how about we start there? Right now."

I'm out of the room and sprinting down the hallway in a breath, only to feel him on my heels, chasing me, and then he's hauling me backward into his arms.

My heart has never felt so full, so complete.

And I know that no matter what the future holds for us, Jackson Pearce will *always* be my Christmas wish.

Want more of Strawberry Hollow and Christmas Spice? Turn the page to read about Parker Grant and his little brother's best friend, Quinn!

chapter one

Quinn

"Quinn, that dress is so lovely on you. It really accentuates your curves. You know, you are such a beautiful girl, and if you only lost a few..." Aunt Polly leans in and whispers, not so quietly, on the other side of her hand, "*pounds,* you would be so breathtaking."

'Tis the damn season.

"Thanks, Aunt Polly, I'm just going to um...get another drink. It was really nice talking to you and catching up. I hope you enjoy the party!" I hold up the almost empty glass flute and offer the best smile I can manage after being insulted directly to my face with her backhanded 'compliment.'

I thought the bright red, festive AF, empire-waist dress made of vintage satin did wonders for my body, but, as always, I'm only the 'pretty' fat girl. The 'you have such a lovely face,' but 'you would be so much prettier if only you were a little thinner' girl. Bringing the glass of champagne to my red-stained lips that match my dress, I down the last of the fizzling liquid and place the empty glass onto a waiter's tray as he passes by me.

While I sometimes miss home, the sleepy, snowy small town that I grew up in, the moment I return, I remember exactly what it was that made me leave Strawberry Hollow in the first place. The small-town gossip, everyone knows everyone kind of town.

Instead of subjecting myself to another 'kind' assault from my family, I grab my faux fur coat, slide it on then head straight for another glass of champagne. The table near the back door is full of glasses, so I swipe two with one hand, giggling to myself when the glass clinks together loudly, and tiptoe toward the patio and make my escape.

Fresh air and copious amount so of champagne are the only way I'm going to make it through this godforsaken Christmas party. The only way I'm going to survive being stuck with my family for the next week and all of their bothersome Christmas festivities is to drink whatever and whenever it's available.

I hate the holidays.

Actually, I *loathe* them.

Like more than anything.

Call me a Scrooge. The Grinch. The girl who hates Christmas.

The fact that I'm even at this stupid party to begin with is only due to the fact that my mother majorly guilt-tripped me into coming home for Christmas this year.

I was perfectly fine hunkering down for another New York winter, watching reruns of Gilmore Girls, and avoiding my family, phone, and email at all costs. The perfect vacation from work. One that I so desperately needed.

But instead, here I am. Enduring an entire seven days with my parents and brother because my mother is on a crusade to bring us all back together for the holidays. Oh, what fun it is...*not*.

Ho-freaking-Ho. Merry my ass.

Thankfully, my Apple Watch shows that it's after eight, which means I can potentially sneak away soon, in a few hours, if I'm lucky. Hopefully, the copious amount of champagne I've consumed so far will make the next hour or two a tad more bearable.

I push open the French doors, letting them fall shut behind me, and step out onto the patio. It's lightly snowing, and cold as a witch's tit out here. But I'm alone, and the silence is a welcome reprieve after the last hour of small talk with extended family members that I can barely remember.

Shaking my head, I set the glasses down on the table. The outdoor dining table and sectional are surrounded by overhead heaters, as well as a massive fire pit in the middle, but that does nothing to stop the bitter cold from creeping in through my coat. Goosebumps erupt on my skin, and I rub my hands together to try and fight off the chill.

It's better than in there, I tell myself.

"Why are you standing out in the freezing cold...in *that*?" From behind me, a deep, gravelly voice interrupts my solitude.

He drags the last word out, laced with arrogance and bravado.

Without turning around, I know exactly who that voice belongs to. The same voice that sends a different kind of shiver down my spine, one that has *absolutely nothing* to do with the cold.

Parker Grant.

Charming playboy, handsome doctor, and the most sought-after bachelor in our hometown.

And...my brother Owen's best friend.

The same guy I've had a crush on since I was a preteen, when he was a gangly, tall teenager only a few years older than me. The guy I doodled in all of my notebooks, my first name with his last, covered in hearts. The first real crush I ever had, and the first one to subsequently break my heart, without him ever knowing.

Years later, and even now, all he has to do is speak and my thighs clench together in unrequited anticipation.

Not that I am still pining away for him. I let go of that silly teenage crush long ago. When I realized that I would never be the kind of girl he was looking for. I was simply his best friend's kid sister who tagged along and annoyed them, any chance I got.

I glance back over my shoulder and see Parker leaning against the pillar in a black sports coat and a tie covered in candy canes around his neck. So sinfully delicious, even with that ridiculous tie that I allow myself a few short seconds to drink him in before I turn back toward the dark tree line and take another hefty sip of champagne, draining half the glass.

"This dress is vintage Valentino, thank you very much."

He laughs, rough and low, and I swallow thickly, feeling it settle in the pit of my stomach.

"The party's inside, and here you are out here...all alone." He comes to stand next to me, resting his thick forearms on the balcony's railing. When he looks over at me, his dark, unruly hair falls across his forehead, and I immediately want to reach out and brush it away. "What's not to enjoy, Quinny?"

The use of my childhood nickname has me squinting my face in disgust. Typical Parker. We used to bicker constantly, he and Owen taking any opportunity they had to tease me.

"Can you not call me that? We're not kids anymore, Parker."

I sway slightly when the wind picks up. His hand darts out to steady me, sliding into my coat as he grips my hip tightly. The warmth of his fingers seep through my dress, and I clear my throat, grabbing onto the rail to ground myself.

"Trust me, I know." The deep, seductive tone catches me by surprise, and I find myself leaning slightly into his touch. His eyes drag down my body slowly, then flit back up to mine.

His eyes burn with intensity. The deep brown of his irises seemingly black in the darkness.

What's happening right now?

I've clearly had too many glasses of champagne.

Is...Parker...flirting with *me*?

No, of course not. *Quinn, no more champagne for you.* Actually, no, maybe I need *more* champagne because I'm clearly losing my mind.

I snap out of it, remembering his question. I tuck my long, dark hair behind my ear and avert my gaze. "I'm out here because I hate the holidays and I hate being home even more. My idea of a good time is not being stuck in a room full of people I barely remember and rarely ever see."

Parker frowns, revealing a shallow line between his dark brows as he does. "You used to love Christmas. You were obsessed with ice skating, decorating the tree. What happened?"

I grew up and realized that life changes in the blink of an

eye. That's what happened. Once my parents divorced and my father moved out, everything changed. My parents hated to be around each other, so that was the end of us all being together.

Our holidays were split. Birthdays. Weekends.

I couldn't wait to leave this town behind, so the second I could, I fled to New York to pursue my career.

I didn't have time to enjoy things like holidays, especially not with my father, who I hardly knew anymore. Not when my only focus has been to advance in my career and make a name for myself.

I shrug, swirling around the remaining champagne at the bottom of my glass. "Life, I guess. I've got exactly zero Christmas spirit, and I'm counting down the seconds until I can board a plane back to what I now call home."

"It's been a while since you've been back home. I mean to Strawberry Hollow at least." His tone is cool and carries a hint of an unasked question.

Exactly four years. But who's counting?

"It has. My mom is on a mission to bring us all back together for the holidays. And you know Stacy…when she gets something in her head, it's happening." I sigh.

Parker laughs, nodding his head in agreement. "Yeah, your mom is definitely tenacious like that. I think it's mostly that she's trying to keep herself busy. Did you know she and the other ladies at the church have put together a caroling group?"

I didn't know that, but in truth, I'm not very close to my mother anymore. When we do talk, our conversations are short and to the point. The fact that Parker knows more about what she's doing than I do…suddenly makes me sad, even if I am part of the reason for the distance between us.

"Sounds like her." I drag my gaze to his and see that he's watching me intently. "What about you? How are things with you?"

The corners of his lips tug up and he shrugs. "Opened my own practice in town, still having dinner with my parents on Sundays. Working on the farm when they need me. Not much has changed since you've left, I guess."

That's partially true. The town has remained mostly the same: small, idyllic, almost untouched by the modernness of the outside world, it seems. But some things *have* changed. Parker, for example.

He's so much taller than I remember. His shoulders fill his jacket in a way that they wouldn't have four years ago, that much I know. It seems like in the time I've been gone, he's turned into a man that I no longer know.

"I always knew that you'd end up opening your own practice. When we were kids, you always took such care cleaning my scrapes and putting band aids on me when I'd fall while riding my bike or scratch myself up, trying to climb into the tree house following you and Owen." I laugh, shaking my head at the memory. Parker Grant spent a lot of time in our house growing up, so most of my memories as a kid include him.

My eyes drift back over his profile as he stares out into the darkness. His nose is slightly crooked from a fight when he was teenager, but if anything, it only makes him even more handsome. A dark brush of stubble is scattered along his jaw, and slightly down his neck. Rugged, yet refined.

Suddenly, he looks over, and I realize I've been caught admiring him.

I'm blaming it on the champagne and not the long-buried crush that's suddenly resurfacing.

"Christmas is magical, Quinn. I know you're a hotshot marketing executive now for a big Fortune 500, but maybe coming home is exactly what you needed, since you've seem to have forgotten that."

Scoffing, I reach for the champagne flute and carefully bring it to my lips for a sip, the bubbles sliding down my throat with ease.

"This *champagne* is magic, Parker. But Christmas? Not so much. I don't know how I'm going to endure the next seven days being stuck at home. Mom is convinced that all we need is quality time together, and that she and Dad are capable of being in the same room without anything being thrown, but I'm calling bullshit. Christmas isn't magic; it's an excuse for people to get presents. Nothing more, nothing less. At least Owen has Cary to act as a buffer."

My brother and his fiancé, Cary, are high school sweethearts, and it's part of the reason he stayed behind in Strawberry Hollow. Now, he has a reason to be absent. Not me. I'm going to be stuck at my parents' beck and call.

"Eh, a week is nothing." His shoulder dips in a shrug. "Maybe you'll find out just how much you miss home now that you're back."

That, I sincerely doubt.

A strong gust of wind disrupts our quiet, seeping through my jacket and causing me to shiver violently. If I stay out here any longer, I'm going to freeze to death.

Clearly, Parker was right to ask why I was standing out in

the cold in this dress and my fashionable, but hardly functional coat. As beautiful as it is, it is not meant for a snowstorm.

I quickly drink the remainder of the champagne in one swallow then set it down on the table. "Thanks for the company. I guess I better head back inside before Mom realizes I'm missing and sends out a search party."

"It was good catching up, Quinny," Parker says, a wistful look in his eyes.

"Yeah, it was," I say softly, our gazes locked. For a moment, neither of us say anything. A moment that suddenly feels intense and overwhelming, and honestly, a little confusing.

These old feelings resurfacing have taken me by surprise. I didn't expect to see him and feel anything but nostalgia.

Somehow, I tear my eyes away, then turn on my heels and walk back through the French doors toward the party. I feel his gaze on me until I slip back inside. The welcomed toasty air greets me, and I sigh, letting it thaw me.

I glance around the room until I spot Owen and Cary cuddled up in the corner, probably whispering sweet nothings in each other's ears. They're so in love, it's sick.

As happy as I am for my brother, I'm also a tad bit...envious?

My love life consists of sporadic Tinder hookups, and that one guy from my building that keeps texting me "you up?" in the middle of the night.

Definitely no fairy-tale romance. Not that I'm looking for Prince Charming.

My job is my life.

My entire world revolves around One Click Marketing.

Trying to make a name for yourself and working your way up the corporate ladder in a male-controlled industry is not easy. It just so happens that my boss is a grade-A misogynistic asshole, who gets off on making women feel inferior. If I hadn't spent the last almost five years of my life building my credibility, I would quit in a heartbeat. But, I'm not giving him the satisfaction of driving yet another woman out.

"Quinn?"

Mom's voice breaks through my thoughts. She's standing in front of me with a glass of creamy liquid, and my mood immediately perks up.

Grandma Scott's famous eggnog.

The one and *only* good thing about Christmas.

"Sorry, I was thinking about work." I plaster on a wide smile, taking the glass from her extended hand. Just what I need to finish out the night.

Hopefully, unscathed, aside from a few fat jabs from Aunt Polly.

Mom's face softens, her eyes wrinkling slightly at the corners. "Quinn, you work too much. See, this is exactly why I wanted you home for Christmas with us. I want all of us together in the same place, enjoying the holiday and not worrying about work or anything else. I just miss you, honey. It's been four years since you've been home." Sadness drips from her tone, matching the expression in her eyes.

I hate when we have these conversations because I feel so immensely guilty. Even though the tension between her and Dad is part of the reason I stopped visiting for the holidays, it still hurts that things between us have gotten so distant. That my need for space continues hurt her.

"I know, Mom. That's why I'm here. All yours for a whole

week. I'm even participating in this Christmas musical, even though I would rather throw myself off the Empire State Building.."

The thought of this damn musical has the champagne ready to come back up.

She perks up, pulling me to her and smashing me against her chest. "I promise, my darling, it's going to be the best vacation ever. Even the musical! I'll make sure of it. Oh, by the way." Pulling back, she smirks and glances to the side.

"See that guy over there? Tall. Blond hair and chiseled jaw?"

I groan, unable to stop it from escaping my lips. "Did you seriously just say *chiseled jaw*? Have you been reading those smutty romance books again?"

"Quinn, hush." The peaks of her cheeks redden with a flush, and I smirk. "It's true, just look at him. He's the definition of chiseled. That's my new neighbor Amelia's grandson, Brent. Isn't he handsome?"

"Oh, no. No, no, no, absolutely not. Mom, you are not setting me up with anyone, ever. Especially not your neighbor's grandson!"

Mom rolls her eyes. "Well, you should at least think about it. You could invite him to dinner tomorrow. Owen invited Parker, and your dad will be coming with his new wife."

Surprisingly, I don't hear the usual thinly-veiled disgust in her mention of my father.

But that means that I don't even get a few days of preparation before we're all thrown together and expected to play nice. My dad's wife is only ten years older than me, and needless to say, I think she probably has more in common with me than with him. Not that I really know anything about her. I only met her once, the night of their wedding.

Following my mom's line of sight, I see the man she's talking about standing across the room with Amelia on his arm. She's not wrong...he is handsome, but regardless, I'm not interested.

I'm here for a week, and my life is not some cliché Hallmark movie, where the corporate girl falls for the sweet, small-town guy when she comes home for Christmas to save the family business or some other contrived festive nonsense.

Nope. Absolutely not happening.

The sooner the holidays can be over and I'm on a plane back to New York, the better.

"I'm just saying, Quinn. You spend too much time working. How will you ever settle down and have a family, if you're always working?" Mom reaches out to affectionately swipe her thumb along my cheek.

"Something tells me that I'll figure it out, Mom. If that's even what I decide I want. But I don't want you or Amelia matchmaking for me, okay? Please."

Finally, she sighs, nodding. "Fine. But dinner is still on. Sorry, sweets."

"Fantastic."

I take a hefty swig of the eggnog and play the part of dutiful daughter, making my way around the room and saying hello to our guests. Before I know it, the crowd has started to disperse, and not a moment too soon since my feet are aching from my new, unbroken-in Louboutins. I walk out of the dining room and into the kitchen, using the doorway to lean on as I pop the heel from my foot.

"Ugh," I moan the moment I can wiggle my freshly-painted toes freely, even though they ache with the movement.

Thank God the party is pretty much over. I'm all 'people'd' out for the night. Actually, for the rest of the year. I'll try again next year.

"I think you lost five inches from those heels."

When I look up, I see Parker has snuck up on me yet again, his hands shoved in the pockets of his slacks, a wry grin on his lips.

"Yeah, well, I was about to lose a toe if I kept those things on any longer," I mutter, sliding the other heel off. "I should've known not to wear heels that haven't been broken in, but I couldn't resist. Did you enjoy the party?"

Parker nods and reaches up, loosening the bright red tie around his neck so that it hangs open. "I did. I love a good party, especially when it's Christmas…"

Only then do I notice the Santa hat shaped cufflinks on his shirt, and I shake my head. "I swear, you are the most Christmas cheer person I've ever met. I don't know how you do it. Thinking about the next week is enough to make my stomach hurt, let alone be *excited*."

"That's because you're obviously the female equivalent of Scrooge, Quinny."

My eyes roll at his teasing, but then I notice what's above us.

Parker notices I'm staring up and his eyes drift to the green leafy plant with red berries directly over our heads.

Wonderful. Could this be any more cliché? In fact, it might possibly be *THE* Hallmark Christmas movie cliché. Just my luck.

"Mistletoe." He grins, stepping closer to me. "You know what this means?"

My heart begins to pound wildly. Surely, he doesn't mean…

He takes another step closer, and I swallow. My fingers tighten their grip around the heel of my shoe while the corners of Parker's lips rise into a full-blown smile that suddenly has my knees feeling weak.

"Sorry, Little Scott, but being the only person around here with real Christmas spirit, you know how important it is to me to follow the holiday traditions. And the mistletoe?" He points above us. "It's one of the most important ones."

I can't kiss Parker. He's…he's Owen's best friend. Not to mention, extremely dangerous for my heart. I can't chance resurrecting those old childhood crush feelings.

"I-"

Before I can even respond, he pulls me to him, sealing his lips over mine and silencing my protest.

Parker Grant is kissing me.

Parker Grant is kissing me!

It takes a second for my brain to catch up to what is actually happening. I think back to all the times that I dreamed of this very moment as a teenager, fantasized about him walking into my room, pulling me into his arms and kissing me until I was breathless.

His lips are firm and demanding, yet soft in a way that is completely unexpected. His hands slide into my hair, pulling me closer against him as his tongue teases the seam of my lips.

Lost in the moment, my heels clatter to the floor, breaking the spell between us.

Parker tears his mouth away and takes a step back.

Stunned, I reach up to touch my swollen and thoroughly kissed lips. I can't believe that just happened.

"You know what, Quinn?" Parker says, closing the space he just put between us. "I bet you, right here, right now, that if you give me these seven days you're home, I can make you fall in love with Christmas all over again."

His words take me back to when we were kids, when everything between us was an adventure, full of fun and games that we loved to play and never got old.

"Really Parker?" I say incredulously.

His shoulder rises in a shrug. "I know you, Quinn Scott, and I know that somewhere in there is the girl that used to wake up with me in the middle of the night, just to see if we could catch Santa. I know that your old Christmas spirit is there, and if you give me a week, just the seven days that you're home, I can make you love those things all over again. Love being *home* again. And if I can't, then I'll take your spot in the Christmas musical your mom has told the entire town you're performing in."

What? Christ on a cracker.

"Hmm. What's the catch?"

Parker shakes his head. "There isn't one. You can hand over the elf costume. Tights and all. That is…if I lose."

Now *this*…is a bet that I'm willing to take. God, not having to dress up in that stupid costume and prance around a stage? I'd do anything.

Well, practically *anything*. Desperate times call for desperate measures, and this is, for sure, a desperate measure.

Or… is it? Maybe I'm only saying yes because I want to

climb Parker like a tree and deal with the consequences later, but either way…

"Deal. Because I know there is absolutely no way that I will ever love this stupid holiday again or love being home….so, you're on. Anything not to put on that stupid costume and be in that horrible play. I'm pretty sure Derick Michaels has worn it four years in a row, and I doubt it's been washed since."

Now this will be entertaining, because there's no possible way I can lose. The odds are fully-stacked against Parker, and I can't wait to revel in my win when I see him on that stage.

"What about you? What if you win, what do you get?" I ask, crossing my arms over my chest.

"If I win, then you're putting on the costume, and that's enough for me, Little Scott."

He grins and adds, "And no cheating. Anything's fair game and you have to give it a *real* shot. I know when you're bullshitting, so no funny business."

"Deal."

"A week from now, we'll meet under the mistletoe at your dad's annual Christmas party, and then we'll see."

There's absolutely no way that Parker Grant and his ridiculous Christmas cheer will be rubbing off or on me. Ever. Which means that I can kiss the ridiculous elf costume and that stupid play goodbye.

Thank God.

"Game on, Dr. Grant."

Keep reading **FREE** in Kindle Unlimited here!

also by maren moore

<u>Totally Pucked</u>
Change on the Fly
Sincerely, The Puck Bunny
The Scorecard
The Final Score
The Penalty Shot
Playboy Playmaker

<u>Orleans University</u>
Homerun Proposal

<u>Standalone</u>
The Enemy Trap
The Newspaper Nanny
The Mistletoe Bet
Jingle Wars

about the author

Top 20 Amazon Bestselling author, Maren Moore writes romantic sports comedies with alpha daddies. Her heroines are best friend material, and you can always expect a HEA with lots of spice. When she isn't in front of her computer writing you can find her curled up with her kindle, binge watching Netflix, or chasing after her little ones.

Be sure to sign up for her newsletter to receive book news FIRST, including exclusive excerpts, giveaways and sales!

Sign up here.